HIS WILD OBSESSION

A WILD BILLIONAIRE ROMANCE

WILD BILLIONAIRE ROMANCE
BOOK 1

C.D. GORRI

HIS WILD OBSESSION

A Billionaire Romance Novel
Wild Billionaire Romance Book 1
By
C.D. Gorri

Copyright C.D. Gorri, NJ 2024

Before you begin sign up for my newsletter here:
SUBSCRIBE HERE

DEDICATION

*For the readers who like book boyfriends that come in
every shade of gray.
I hope you enjoy Sofia and Adrik's story.
Xoxo,
C.D. Gorri*

These wild billionaire playboys are used to getting their way...

There isn't much money can't buy, especially when it comes to pleasure. But can these curvy women tame these billionaire beasts and win their love? Or will their souls be sucked into oblivion by the wanton bliss their bodies crave more and more with every surrender?

Each of our heroes wears a mask on the outside to face the world, but his disguise comes off when he runs into the one female who makes his blood run hot. Need and possessive passion abound in these books, but our heroes know only one way to control their desires.

Will they f*ck the feeling they see as weakness out of

their systems, or will their needs only grow more wild with every touch, kiss, and plunge into ecstasy with the object of his affections?

Our Billionaire Heroes

Adrik Volkov
Marat Volkov
Josef Aziz
Andres Ramirez

Trigger Warnings
(I have never done one of these, so please forgive me if I muck this up.)
This series has profanity, graphic steamy scenes, voyeurism, violence, deceased parents, alcoholism (not the MCs), misogyny (not the MCs), questionable morals, manipulations, fake relationships, revenge, and romantic obsessions that may be unhealthy.

This is fictional. This is not real life.
Always take care of your mental, emotional, and physical self because you are important.

He's a hardened ex-criminal. She's a stranger to his world.

Adrik Volkov worked hard to wipe the slate clean of his criminal past for his sake and his brother's. Bringing Volkov Industries into the 21st century has taken everything he's got. But it's been worth it. His company's patented mining techniques for harvesting rare earth metals used in electronics and smart tech have made him a billionaire.

Instead of breaking legs and taking names, he's attending parties with people he neither likes nor understands. It's all part of his new title. But money can't erase his harsh upbringing. Once a brawler, always a brawler. Those skills come in handy when he sees a woman being accosted at one of the ritzy, booze filled gatherings he must attend.

Sofia DiFalco was more than just a damsel in distress. The curvy stranger made his body buzz with desire and his hard heart beat a little faster. From the second he saw her, Adrik wanted only one thing. *Sofia in his bed.* But after one tantalizing night, she disappears without a trace.

He tries to forget her, but she's an obsession, and he just can't let go.

CHAPTER ONE
ADRIK

The party was filled with A-listers, billionaires, tech gurus, and the usual high class smorgasbord of sin and temptations. I was bored.

"Ad, why don't you have a drink?" Marat, my younger brother asked.

His dark eyes were twinkling with mischief as he raised his glass of champagne, toasting a group of waifish runway models who could not stop looking at him. I don't blame them. Marat is a handsome man. Not me.

Not that I was ugly, but I looked hard, *unkind*, was the correct word. But they should know a man like me would not be inclined to show kindness. Not in my business. Well, former business. I kept forgetting we were legitimate now.

Volkov Industries used patented mining techniques for harvesting rare earth metals used in electronics and smart tech. We led the industry and held many claims overseas in areas where it was necessary to have brains, money, and guns to secure mining rights. Good thing I had all those and more.

"I don't drink bubble piss like you, Marat," I replied, and my brother tossed his head back and laughed out loud.

Bloody hell. Even his laughter was attractive. Like angels frolicking gaily from above. I rolled my eyes just as the throng of barely dressed stick figures walked over to see if they could catch his attention. Likely they could. But only for an evening.

My brother was a dyed in the wool bachelor. There was no changing that tiger's stripes. Pity. I would have liked to be an uncle someday. Children were the future, and far as I was concerned, the Volkov name would not continue from my loins.

Nyet.

I would not marry. I would never have children. After all the horror and evil I had seen that humanity was capable of, how could I? Besides, there was no woman in my life. No one woman, anyway. Yes, I took women to bed. I was a red-blooded man. Fucking was as good an outlet as violence, and since we were legit, well, violence seldom came my way anymore. But I meant there was no one who had a claim on my affections. I did not believe in love. And my lovers knew the deal.

Make no demands. Come when I say so. Leave immediately after.

That was the only way a woman made it to my bed. She had to agree to my terms, and few refused me. Whether it was the size of my bank account or my cock that made them say yes, who cared? Both were larger than the average man, and I never heard any complaints.

"Ladies, are you enjoying yourselves?" Marat started chatting up the women, and I growled in disgust.

"The balcony seems empty, boss. If you need some air."

Josef, our head of security, handed me a tumbler of Whiskey Neat, the platinum label, before pointing to my sanctuary. I grunted and accepted the heavy, squat glass before I stood up.

"Thank you, Josef. I'll leave you and Marat to these women," I murmured, taking a swallow before walking away.

The penthouse had been checked out by my security team upon my arrival and the six-man unit was still afoot, checking perimeters and making sure my brother and I were safe, and the area secured. Yes, we were out of the gangster game, but that did not mean we did not have enemies.

In fact, I'd seen legitimate corporations commit positively heinous acts that made mobsters look like pussycats. Espionage, strong arming, short selling, lying, bribery, blackmail, and outright murder. And those were just some of what we've encountered since we purportedly left the crime world.

"Volkov, is it?"

A slimy looking man with white hair combed back, wearing a silk shirt and crisp wool pants stood in front of me. I did not accept his proffered hand. In fact, I did not say anything. I merely gave him the dead eyed stare that had made better men than he piss themselves on more than one occasion.

"Um, I was very excited to hear you would be attending this little shindig, Volkov. You know I think you and I should talk business—"

I walked away before he could finish, knowing Josef was watching me and would waylay the man before he even thought to follow me. That was why I allowed Josef to stay on as head of security even after he'd made his first mint.

Marat and I did not agree on a lot, but we both insisted on rewarding those who helped us when we were scraping by at the bottom of the barrel. It wasn't so long ago that we were two orphaned boys running around the streets of Moscow. Our Italian mother had been killed alongside our father in some ugliness involving drugs. He was a low level Bratva soldier, and we were left with nothing but the clothes on our backs.

When I turned sixteen, I was already more muscular than most adult men and I used it to my advantage, picking fights with gang members and robbing the robbers. They called me the wolf because of the way I worked. I was known for being a hunter, patient, stalking my prey, even toying with them before the end. Once I let them see me, that end was inevitable.

No one survived the wolf. It was fitting since Volkov literally meant wolf. I liked it. Liked the terror it struck in men's hearts when they heard the dark wolf was coming for them. Taking over territory was easy after that. By the time we left Russia, I was already in control of my own set of illegal trade routes. New York City was like a playground after that.

That was over twenty years ago. I just had my thirty-seventh birthday, and as of six months ago, Volkov Industries had gone completely legitimate. Still, I missed the solitude that came with being one of the world's most feared men. I did not have to attend parties like this one where I stuck out like a sore thumb despite my custom suit and four thousand dollar shoes.

These businessmen were lean and had soft hands. Their bellies never knew hunger. Their eyes were blind to what was around them. They did not see the wolf in their midst. Even the ones who claimed to know me did not know. They couldn't possibly comprehend what kind of monster they were rubbing elbows with.

I finished my drink and stood on the balcony, sucking in the fresh air despite the chill. It was a damn sight better than the heavily perfumed party room, which still could not cover up the stink of humanity's so-called upper classes. To me, nothing smelled worse than avarice and greed. The people inside had no souls. They thought they were better than men like me.

I shook my head. It was dangerous for my

thoughts to turn so dark. I needed a new project, something to focus on. And it was while I thought about the emails sitting on my laptop that I glanced to the side and saw something out of the corner of my eye.

Two enormous potted plants decorated with tiny lights sat in one corner of the large balcony over-looking the city. I supposed it was festive, as it was just after the long holiday season. But really, I did not care about fairy lights and horticulture.

It was the creature beyond the plants that intrigued me. Swatches of pale skin bathed in silver caught my eye. Like liquid moonlight teased me from behind those very plants. I did not recognize her. She sure as fuck did not look like the other women there.

Her back was to me, but I saw her pale, smooth skin, and dark hair quite clearly. She was round and lush, with plenty of curves and valleys I was tempted to explore. I wanted to see her face, but as I inched closer, I realized she was not alone.

In fact, she looked as though she was trying to get away from whoever had her cornered, but between the balcony and the plants, she had nowhere to go. She looked stunning in the tight silver dress she wore, but I was not in the habit of gaping at women in public. Especially women engaged in uncomfortable situations with their dates.

I was also not accustomed to playing knight in shining armor, but if the man making her uncomfortable did not stop, well, like I said, I was bored. So, I edged closer, leaning in to listen to the couple, if that was what they were.

"No, thank you," the woman said firmly.

I could tell she meant it, her whole posture was like a bright red stop sign. The idiot talking to her had no clue. He was some slick talking old man with too much money, and not enough scruples. Seeing her tense as she pushed his hand off her arm incensed me. I had not experienced such a fierce reaction to a stranger before. Interesting, but not enough to move me.

Yet.

"You say no, but I think you really mean yes, doll. Am I right, or am I right?"

"No, I really mean no," she said, but the man only stepped closer. "Look, um, I'm not here alone."

"Don't try that line with me. Come on. Who'd you come with? Now I have a room downstairs, and it will be just me and you," the old man said, forcing her back another step.

She had nowhere to go and as the bastard pushed himself against her body and moved in for a kiss I reacted. What could I say? I really did not like him touching her.

"I suggest you step away from my date," I growled softly, coming out from behind the plant to stand beside the woman.

Soft brown eyes looked up at me, surprised but she caught on quickly, lacing her arm through mine and pressing her body into my side, seeking comfort. At least, I liked to think so.

"There you are, darling," she said and smiled.

"I am sorry I took too long. Who is your friend," I said the last word with disdain.

"Look pal, I don't know who you think you are, some Euro trash fucker, but I was talking to this lady. My name is Henry Devain," he said, and I recognized the name.

"Ah, Councilman Devain. Yes, I know you. I wonder if your constituents would want to know about your penchant for pressuring young women at parties? Young women who very clearly told you they were with someone else."

The woman in question gasped, and I realized she did not recognize Mr. Devain. Interesting. I wondered what she was doing at the party. Who was she?

She was certainly beautiful, but with a round ass and pair of breasts that were definitely natural. She did not belong to the group of models my brother preferred, nor was she one of the plastic dolls the other wealthy men had on their arms. My cock hardened behind my zipper, and need pulsed through me.

Yes. I wanted her in my bed, and I planned to get her there. Just as soon as this asshole walked away. Though, it really was a shame I was not in the leg breaking business anymore.

"Who the fuck do you think you are, mister?" Devain snarled.

"You know, I have lived in New York for twenty years now, and English is ooh, my third or fourth language, but I am still amused by the American colloquial preference to add fuck to the middle of every utterance. As if such a thing made you a hard man. Do you think you are a hard man, Mr. Devain?" I asked.

"What? Who are you, buddy?"

He put his hand on my shoulder as he asked his question again. Even the woman tensed, knowing that was a mistake. Still, I liked the feel of her on my arm and against my side, and I had no wish to move her out of the way. So, I didn't. Faster than he could register, I had his hand off my suit and twisted in a way that made the little man yelp in pain.

"I am Adrik Volkov," I said, and the man paled.

Then I used my leverage to bring Devain to his knees before turning to the woman.

"Do you want me to hurt him?" I asked.

She looked at me, her brown eyes going, if possible, even wider, and she shook her head. My pulse sped up, but outwardly, I remained passive. Showing nothing was a specialty of mine honed from years of living hard.

"No. Thank you, but I am fine. You got here before he could do anything."

I nodded. A part of me was disappointed, but another part was thrilled. I let this woman, this stranger, see the wolf, and yet she still clung to my arm. Still looked at me with soft eyes.

I wondered what else was soft about her.

"Want to leave this place?" I asked, staring down at her.

Electricity sizzled between us. It happened like that sometimes. Attraction, raw and primal, rose in a man in times of intense emotion or confrontation. Such as this one, though the conflict was small. Still, my dick was hard, and she was so beautiful. I wanted her, but I was not like this man. I would ask. And only then would I proceed or not. Long seconds ticked by, but then she nodded.

"Don't misunderstand. I am asking you to go someplace else. Someplace to be alone with me, Zaika," I said, calling her a bunny in my native tongue.

She was like that to me, bathed in moonlight and silver silk. I wanted to hunt her down. Sink my teeth into her soft skin.

"I understand," she said, and nodded again. "And I am still saying yes, Mr. Volkov."

She was playing with fire. A dangerous game, but I was not about to tell her that. I just kept her arm in mine and walked away from the crying politician. The little bunny had no idea she'd just said yes to the big bad wolf.

CHAPTER TWO
SOFIA

I don't know why I even went to that party. My boss had assured me she needed me with her. Working as a personal assistant to one of Manhattan's buzzing socialites was exhausting, but I finally had enough information to finish the novel I'd been working on since I'd graduated from college.

Missy Castle told me I would be by her side all evening, but after half an hour rubbing elbows with the elite, the hairbrained woman disappeared behind closed doors, leaving me to fend for myself. I didn't mind at first. The book I was writing was a romantic suspense and my characters were based on tabloid darlings just like the people attending that shindig.

The borrowed dress I wore fit me like a second

skin. I never wore clothes that tight. Not with my ass, which I unfortunately inherited from my Grandma Rose.

Thanks a lot, Nonna.

But the slinky silver material felt like silk against my skin, and it was the only chance I would likely ever get to attend a party where I'd be sure to see politicians, athletes, moguls, and movie stars in the same room. My poor little Jersey girl heart could hardly stand it. But I managed not to drool on anyone, so there was that.

Of course, I also managed to get myself cornered by some white-haired creep. You would think with age came scruples, but apparently that meant jack shit to this fella. He was so slimy, pressing up against me and backing me into a corner, which was admittedly my own fault. I should have paid attention to where I was going.

I was about sixty seconds from smacking the man upside the head, also thanks to Grandma Rose who taught me a long time ago how to defend myself from unwanted advances. I usually kept a roll of nickels in my bag when I went out for such occasions as this. Only, well, the coat check girl had offered to keep my purse safe, and I didn't think I would need it in such a place.

Just goes to show you, there were dogs every-where. I tried to get out of the situation with some tact, not wanting to offend whoever the creepy little man was, and good thing too. Turned out he was a politician, likely with resources I could not even begin to imagine.

Anyway, Councilman Creep, as I'd dubbed him, sort of had his ass handed to him by the sexiest, and most dangerous looking man I had ever seen in my entire life. I almost lost balance looking up into the face of the man who'd come to my rescue. Holy crap. He was tall. Like Khal Drogo tall.

I never knew real people came in that size. And his shoulders. Christ. He had to turn his body into mine so we could fit through the balcony door, even though he'd already pushed me to walk in front of him. I was stunned by his masculine beauty. Features like his belonged on statues guarding citadels. Fierce, proud, lethal, and when he looked at me—hot.

I was no blushing virgin, and I knew when a man wanted me. Moisture pooled between my legs as my interest stirred for the sexy stranger. He smelled like cologne. It was something spicy, exotic, and expen-sive, I could not tell what brand or name.

He paused a moment by two men and said a few

words in what I thought was Russian or some kind of Eastern European. I was terrible at languages. Both strangers were tall and imposing. One was ridiculously handsome, and he seemed surprised, but seemed to approve if the way he winked at me meant anything. The other merely nodded, like an employee would. Neither did a thing for me.

How could they? Neither man was *him*. My tall, powerful, sexy rescuer. He'd said his name was Adrik Volkov. I racked my brain for more. I did not have a photographic memory, but it was close enough that I could recall things if I really tried.

Volkov. Volkov?

Could it be? I recalled the name Volkov Industries. I'd seen it before likely when reading a newspaper or magazine while I searched for fodder for my novel. The company had a silver wolf as their logo with bright red eyes, which was why I remembered it oh so vividly. It reminded me of something supernatural. I was a sucker for shows like Game of Thrones, True Blood, Bitten, and countless others.

I had no idea what they did, and I did not know enough about Russian names to know if it was a common one. Volkov could be like Smith for all I knew. I supposed Adrik Volkov could be a relative to whoever ran Volkov Industries.

But that was unlikely. Besides, it didn't really matter to me. Whatever this was, it was one night only. My entire focus was on keeping myself upright in the stupid heels I was wearing and walking straight. God knew, my knees were knocking just from the way his thumb rubbed the inside of my elbow.

Was I really going to do this?

Casual sex was not part of my daily vocabulary, but I had to admit no one had ever tempted me like this before. His heavy-lidded gaze stayed on me as we got in the elevator. I watched as he swiped his keycard then hit a secret button behind a silver plate.

"We're going up? I thought this was the penthouse."

"This is *a* penthouse, Zaika. I own *the* penthouse."

There was a difference. And I learned what it was the second the elevator opened the opposite from where we'd entered. Gleaming wood floors, expensive, sleek furniture. But nothing compared to the dazzling view of New York City through the floor to ceiling windows that made up the entire front wall.

"Oh my," I whispered, stunned into silence.

Central Park, Columbus Circle, everything looked so close yet so small. I could even see clear to the Hudson River. Nerves assailed me for the first time since I was in his presence, and it was all because of one body of water. My entire life I tried to get away from my humble beginnings, but there it was, staring me right in the face.

It wasn't that I was ashamed of where I came from. I had a great family. One of those huge Italian clans where the grandparents came over after the war and bought a building or two back in the 50s in North Bergen. They still owned it, though Grandpa Paolo died when I was in high school.

Most of my family still lived there, my father included. Mama passed just two years ago, and he was still buried in a bottle with Nonna looking after him. No, I wasn't ashamed, but it was a long way from Kennedy Boulevard to Billionaire's Row.

"You want a drink?" he asked, and I noticed his accent was a little more pronounced than it had been earlier.

In fact, I hadn't noticed a trace of it until he'd asked me if I wanted him to hurt that creep. I knew it shouldn't have turned me on, but it did. I was used to fighting my own battles, but it was nice to know chivalry was not dead.

"Um, sure," I replied, accepting the glass of wine he held out.

"Should we toast to something?"

"How about knights in, well, I was going to say shining armor, but tailored tuxes has a nice ring, doesn't it?" I replied.

"This is a suit, not a tuxedo."

He took a sip of what I thought might be whiskey before placing it on a very chic glass table. He took my wine glass from my hand after I'd sipped the rich, sweet liquid, and placed it beside his glass. Then he stepped closer, invading my space.

"I know. Um, are you always so literal?" I asked, trying not to wince at how breathless I sounded.

"Understanding things is very important to me. I do not like for there to be miscommunications. This dress, is it yours?" he asked.

"That's a strange question," I said, frowning.

"I ask because the straps are too big. If it were yours, I'd suggest you find a new seamstress or tailor," he whispered.

He ran his fingers across my neck, tracing my clavicle, and up over my shoulder, lifting the strap I'd been toying with half the night. One tug and the thing fell down. He treated the other side to more of the same, and by that time my eyes were half closed as I swayed towards him.

"Your skin is like silk, Zaika. I would like to see more of it."

I don't know when he started kissing me, but honestly, once our mouths met it was like fireworks went off, planets collided, and maybe whole universes were created with that simple joining of lips. I'd had quite an enthusiastic Physics teacher in high school. The woman sure loved to lecture about atoms.

"So soft," he growled into my mouth, and every brain cell I had just incinerated.

Next, we were moving against each other. Hands roamed, clothing came off, mouths crashed together, teeth nipped, and I moaned, leaning into every caress and pet he offered. The room was heated, but goosebumps broke out across my skin as he bent down and removed my dress.

"So beautiful," he groaned, stepping back, and staring at me as I stood before him in nothing but my heels.

I trembled, awareness spiking. It didn't seem to matter to him that I carried an extra thirty pounds or so, especially in my breasts, hips, and ass. In fact, the big, sexy Russian seemed to like those parts of me best. My soft belly and thick thighs didn't put him off, and when he reached for me, I felt his desire like it was a living thing.

He walked backwards till he was sitting on the

edge of the sofa, keeping me standing before him like some sort of pagan sacrifice. I grabbed onto his head as his lips explored my sensitive body. He sucked my nipples into his hot mouth, biting the tips. I moaned louder, arching my back in an effort to get closer to him.

The heat between us increased another ten degrees, and my sex throbbed and clenched, needing something more. As if he knew exactly what I wanted, my sexy soon to be lover growled out some words in Russian and bit my skin, trailing his tongue down my belly and towards the apex of my thighs.

Even standing in front of him in high heels, with him sitting down on the couch, he was so tall Adrik had to lean over to get to my goodies. Fucking hell, it felt so good when his big tongue lapped at my seam. He put his hands on my thighs, spreading my legs so he could access my now dripping core and I almost lost it right then and there.

It was crazy, foolish, reckless of me to let him continue. Completely wild, and unusual behavior. But maybe that was why I didn't stop him. How many times in my life was a man like him going to treat me like I was some kind of sex goddess?

Once. Exactly once. And that was why when he picked me up, his big body leaning back as he draped my legs over his shoulders so I could ride his face, I did not hesitate. I was completely on board with Adrik Volkov's plans to make every carnal fantasy I've ever had come true that night.

Still, I was reticent at first. Shy because of my weight and the fact I was pretty damn new to this. But he offered no reprieve as his mouth latched onto my clit with merciless intent. A second later, he speared my entrance with two thick fingers, stretching my channel and stroking me deeper than any man's hands ever had.

"Fuucck," I groaned, my entire system going into hyper drive.

"Not yet," he growled against my clit.

By that time, my hips were thrusting by themselves as I chased my orgasm. But bastard that he was, he wouldn't let me come. He brought me to the edge, only to deny me completion. For that, I pulled his hair harder. I grabbed at his shoulders too, my nails scratching at him to get better leverage, but his firm hand stopped me.

"Not yet, Zaika. You come when I say, not before," he grunted against my thigh.

"Please," I begged, needing to finish what he started.

He pulled me off his shoulders, sitting me astride

his lap but putting some inches of space between us. I was so close. Frustration made me whimper. It was all I could do not to reach down with my fingers and get myself off, but something told me Adrik wouldn't like that, so I bit my lip and moaned while he undid his fly. Not his button, just his fly. Strange, I thought as I watched him take a condom from his pocket and unwrap it from my position on his lap.

Next, he reached inside his pants and took out his cock. My mouth dropped open. I'd seen naked men before, but not in his class. He was thick and long, heavily veined, and I watched with rapt attention as he gave himself a long hard stroke before rolling the condom on.

"Like what you see, Zaika?"

Oh, my freaking God. Yes. I liked. I liked it a lot, but I was speechless.

"Climb on," he instructed, and I did.

Raising myself to my knees, I moved, closing the space between us. I was so hungry for him, I couldn't get enough. The idea of fucking him in nothing but my heels while he was still dressed was so damn erotic, I felt even more of my arousal gathering at my sex, readying me for his sweet invasion.

"Oh God," I moaned when he lifted me by the hips, just enough to position his dick at my entrance.

"Now, Zaika," he commanded, and I pushed down, taking him in one hard thrust.

We both moaned, and I gasped, unable to catch my breath. He was so big and thick. It burned where he stretched me even though I was already so hot and wet, needy for him. I didn't think I could take it, but then he was whispering to me in Russian, kissing my neck and running his hands all over my body.

"Let me in, Zaika. Ride my cock. Use my body to make you feel good," he whispered seductively.

His honeyed words had me moaning, and soon I was moving, taking from him everything he told me to. I wanted to come. I wanted to use his body to make mine sing. His fingers bit into the flesh over my hips and ass, and it felt so good I could not stop my moaning if I tried. The rustle of fabric as we worked together was erotic in the otherwise silence of the room. It felt good against my sensitive skin. Just something else to add to my already overstimulated senses.

"That's it, faster, Zaika. Come for me, now," he grunted.

His voice was so deep, it was like the vibrations struck a nerve within me. He slapped my ass, squeezing the cheeks and pressing me down harder. Fuck. He was so deep. So deep.

My entire body began to tremble and shake, and then I was coming harder than I ever came before. Adrik roared, his face buried in my neck as he thrust jerkily from beneath me, and I knew he was coming too.

I tried to catch my breath, uncertain of the protocol for after you finished fucking a man like that. I had no idea what came next. But I didn't have to worry yet because apparently, we were not done.

Adrik picked me up, his cock still buried deep inside my well-used pussy, and he walked with me in his arms to the bedroom. He kissed me hard, shrugging off his jacket and shirt without breaking contact. His kisses wrecked me. They were so thorough and intense. He made me feel like I was the only woman in the world, and I wondered briefly how many women he had to kiss to learn how to do that.

No, I was not going there. I shook the thoughts from my brain and concentrated on the now. His tongue tangled with mine, chasing doubts away as he cupped my cheeks and held onto my face like he was starving, and I was a fount of nourishment. Only when he wanted to remove his pants did he slide out of my sex, still hard and ready.

He exchanged the used condom for a new one,

taking off his shoes and pants and gracing me with a delectable view of his incredible ass. His entire back was covered in tattoos, the most prominent of which was a lone black wolf with red eyes howling at the moon.

My body went haywire just looking at him. Covered in rippling muscles, he was the most devastatingly gorgeous man I had ever seen. He was not some pretty boy. And something told me he'd worked hard to get where he was. Maybe that was why I was so attracted to him. I felt a sort of connection to him, and not just because of what we were doing together.

"Eyes on me, Zaika. I want you here when I fuck you, not somewhere else in your mind."

I smiled before pulling him down to meet my eager mouth. He caged me in, making me feel safe and tiny, which was a really hard fucking thing to do, but he managed. His body dwarfed mine, and when he moved his hips, finding my sex with his with unerring accuracy, I knew I was going to save tonight in my memories for a long time. Possibly forever.

"Greedy little thing, aren't you? So hungry for my cock."

"You feel so good inside me, Adrik. You have me wild for you."

"Is that so?" he asked, grinning wickedly as he stopped moving his body and pulled his head out of reach, denying me his lips. "Tell me what you want."

"What?" I asked, unsure of how to play that little game.

"Tell me what you want me to do, Zaika, or I will stay just like this," he said, and I groaned in frustration.

"I want you to move."

"Move how? For what purpose?"

"I want you to fuck me, Adrik. I want you to make me come again."

"I see," he growled, moving his hips slowly at first. "Like this?" he asked.

"No. I want you deeper, harder. Stop messing around and fuck me like before," I said, the demand in my voice surprising even myself.

"You have teeth, don't you, little Zaika?"

Adrik grunted. His black eyes glittered in the darkness like obsidian. He tugged on my lower lip with his thumb and pointer finger. Then he lowered his hand to wrap around my neck, withdrawing almost all the way before slamming his hips to mine and filling me in one hard, pounding thrust. It felt so damn good, I almost came right then.

Good sex was not something I was used to getting on a regular basis. In fact, it had been over a year since I had sex of any kind, and this was better than that. Better than any regular old sex.

This was wild, unadulterated, multi-orgasmic, off the rails, slay me now sex. I didn't know how I was ever going to look at another man after what Adrik was doing to me tonight. But I'd find a way because I was not stopping either. I was in it for the duration.

I would deal with the consequences tomorrow.

CHAPTER THREE
ADRIK

The first thing I remembered when I woke up was the taste of Zaika moya. Poor little thing, I'd kept her up till the sun rose with my insatiable hunger for her. I could not help myself.

Her pussy was like ambrosia. Better than any drug or alcohol, or that Swiss chocolate Josef was addicted to. It was the best damn thing I had ever had. It was like fucking pure moonlight. Ever do that? Fuck the moon?

That was what it felt like to be buried between her legs. From the moment I saw her in that silver dress that was not hers, I wanted her. And now that I'd had her, I wanted her still. More, even.

But when I opened my eyes, Zaika moya was

gone. I sat up, tossing the rumpled sheets aside before checking the bathroom attached to my bedroom. Next, I searched the common rooms of the penthouse. But no. She was gone.

The silver dress. My moonlight goddess. Zaika moya. Gone. Fuck.

"Motherfucker," I growled and ran my hands over my face.

I didn't even get her name. Fuck. The scent of coffee told me Josef was in the kitchen. I did not like a lot of people in my space. Sure, there were guards outside, but the cleaning staff was ordered to come when I was not in residence.

Josef, of course, would let himself in whenever he wanted. I had gotten used to the man's coffee, and you could say I was addicted. No one made a pour over like him. As for my brother, he had his own place, but with the party last night being in the same building, I was not surprised he'd stayed over. Right then, I did not give two shits for Josef or Marat. Not even when my brother opened his bedroom door and escorted three scantily clad women to the front door.

"Ad, if you are going to parade around naked at least wait for my dates to leave so they don't think they went home with the wrong brother," Marat joked, tossing me a towel as the giggling trio of women looked their fill.

I snarled, and they stopped laughing, leaving fast as their stilettos would carry them. Usually, I was better behaved than that. But I was out of sorts, admittedly so. I'd never felt that way about a woman, especially one I had just met.

But there was something so right in the way we came together last night. It was like she saw my soul. All the dark damaged pieces of me, and she wanted me anyway. How the fuck could I have let her go without getting her name? Woman must have fucked me into a stupor. I never slept that well.

"Boss?" Josef handed me a mug of coffee, steaming and black, like I liked it.

"I want you to find her, Josef."

"Who?"

"The woman from last night," I growled.

He knew damn well who I meant. But my head of security just raised his eyebrows and shrugged.

"I already tried, Adrik. But she was not on the guest list and our host did not recognize her."

"Did you see her leave?"

"No. I would not have allowed it. Or I would have sent her home in a car or something, so we knew where to reach her. Just in case. But the new men, they did not think," he explained, but I was too angry to care.

"Fire them. I cannot have imbeciles working for me."

"Fire them?"

"Move them, then. Somewhere else. Far away from me. I need guards who are aware at all times," I growled.

"Yes, boss."

Josef nodded. He'd tried to convince me to hire men from the old days, but I'd been determined to break ties. Unfortunately, my head of security was right about this. Even heads of corporations had enemies. If my guards would allow a single woman to walk past them unattended and unquestioned, then they needed to be replaced.

"Is this about the woman from last night?" Marat asked, joining us with a mug of coffee and looking like some sort of male angel in his white silk robe.

"Who needs women with you looking so pretty?" Josef teased, and Marat frowned.

"Fuck off, Josef. So, big brother, you got lucky?" he goaded. "She was pretty. A little thick for my tastes, especially in the ass department, but whatever gets you hard—ouch!"

I did not bother answering with words, just

cuffed Marat in the back of the head like I used to when we were kids.

"Fuck, Ad. You didn't have to hit me," he grumbled, messing with his hair.

I ignored him and just kept staring out the window. It was a multimillion dollar view, but all I saw was her. Her eyes when she turned them up at me as I undressed her delectable body. Her lips when they parted, screaming my name as I pushed us both over the edge of ecstasy.

But even more than the sex, was her conversation. Between bouts of lovemaking and hard core fucking, yes, we had engaged in both, we'd talked. She was smart. Funny. And I was a fucking idiot for not getting her name.

It was like I was under some damned witch's spell. I felt obsessed with the woman. And that was not okay for a man like me.

"Why do you look so grim, Ad? You got lucky last night. Smile, for fuck's sake," Marat said, continuing the discussion when I would much rather stew in silence.

"Lucky? No. It was not lucky. Whoever that woman was, she bewitched me, Marat. I need to find her."

"Find her? What the fuck are you talking about?" my brother asked, seemingly stunned.

He was not wrong. I never got this way over a woman. Sex was easy for men like me, with money, power, and it was not bold to say I had a certain appeal. I was not pretty like Marat, but I was fit, and my face was far from ugly. But there was something about my Zaika that got under my skin. Something that made me want more than I should.

"Josef, I mean it. Find her."

"Yes, boss," he replied again, and I knew my orders would be followed.

Marat stood up, his face a study in disbelief. My poor pretty brother could not understand why a woman held me so captive. Maybe it was because it took three to satisfy him. But Zaika was enough to fill any man's most desperate desires—a thought that spiked primordial rage through my blood.

No one should have access to her sweet body but me. No, she had not been a virgin when I took her on the couch, then my bed. I learned so many of her secrets last night. But not all of them. Still, as far as I was concerned, Zaika moya was unfuckingtouched by all save me.

My proprietary instincts were off the charts, and

I knew it was absolutely insane of me. To feel ownership over this female. To crave her like I craved oxygen. Not as an extra, but as a necessity. It was madness. Especially since I knew so little about her.

"Adrik, we need your head focused on business," my brother said.

Suddenly, he was standing in front of me. And I hadn't even heard him move. That was unlike me. I was used to being the wolf, the hunter, the apex predator tracking every breath my prey expelled. And everyone was my prey. Everyone.

Especially her.

"This merger with CoreTech, you remember? The company working on the drill we need for our new mines is important. We need this win, Ad. It will be far cheaper to just buy some pussy to keep you entertained until the deal is done." Marat said, clearly exasperated.

I sucked air between my teeth and let loose a low growl. Marat was my brother, and I loved him, but if he spoke about Zaika moya one more time, I'd beat the shit out of him. The topic was off limits to everyone, and I supposed I needed to lay down some ground rules.

"I know what needs to be done, Marat. I have

been taking care of business, of you, of me, longer than perhaps you remember."

"I know, Adrik. I know. I just never saw you affected like this by some slu—"

"Do not finish that word," I warned.

"I'm s-sorry," Marat gasped, and I released my grip on his throat.

Fuck. I didn't even realize I had grabbed him until I was already letting go. I shook my head and clenched my fists at my side.

"The woman is not your concern. I will have Josef find her and I will do what I need to do. Fuck her out of my system. Then I will get on with business as usual," I growled, then snapped my attention to our head of security. "Tell me the moment you find her."

"Yes, boss. I am on it."

"Good," I growled, stalking back to my bedroom.

I hated to wash off her scent, like jasmine, sweet, sultry, and fruity, but I needed to shower. Business never rested, and I had many responsibilities. I remembered the slimy councilman from last night and made a note to tell Josef to start with questioning him about Zaika moya.

I need to know her real name. Where she lives. Who she is. I want every bit of information I can get about her.

Information was power. And I had always been at my happiest when I held all the cards.

Once dressed in another custom suit made of the softest wool, of which I had dozens, I met Josef and Marat in the living room. They were also similarly dressed and ready to go to the new Volkov building we bought and renovated.

Old habits die hard, and I absently patted the place where I used to keep my knife and gun. Even with special holsters designed so weapons would not be recognizable, I could not get past security in most of the higher end office buildings armed.

Besides, I was a businessman now. Not a criminal. A distinction that was hardly visible on most days. Maybe there was something to be said for the way I grew up. Everything I had, I worked for. This place, these people. They did not understand that kind of grit.

CoreTech was owned by one of the New York elites I so often found myself in meetings and parties with these days. The Castle family was old money, and while they enjoyed power, they were not hungry for it. In fact, they never knew real hunger. I walked into the new Volkov Towers with a determination I hadn't felt in years.

I had a meeting with Matthew Castle in an hour.

After that, Josef would likely have an update on Zaika moya. Until then, I would focus my energy on doing what I did best, hunting down what it was Mr. Castle really wanted. Then, I would offer it in exchange for the company I needed for our newly acquired mines.

"Marat, Andres will be adding some events to your calendar for the next couple of weeks. Make sure you are available," I told my brother, naming my assistant.

I just then decided to devote the next few days to my unusual task. Vacation was not a word in my vocabulary, and this was hardly the time, but as the minutes passed by, I became keenly aware I was missing something. I was missing her. And that would not do.

"Of course, brother. May I ask, where will you be?" Marat asked casually.

It seemed he'd already forgiven me for my outburst. Not that I would apologize. He deserved the reminder of what I really was. Maybe all the luxury surrounding us had caused a lapse in his memory. But we'd been raised hard. And even though his almost too good-looking face was made even prettier with his straight-toothed, brilliant white smile, I saw the darkness in his nearly black eyes. No, my baby brother did not need reminding. He knew exactly who I was.

Wolf.

I raised an eyebrow, glaring at him until he shrugged and tossed his hands up in surrender. Marat had everything I ever wanted for him, but sometimes I wondered if he wasn't as lonely as I was. Two wolves did not make a Pack, and yet we were not ever alone, having only each other in this vast, cruel world.

I would do anything for my brother, and I have. I did not doubt his loyalty for a second, but I wanted him busy when *she* was found. Last thing I needed was to compete with him for the attentions of a woman who'd left my bed like it was on fire.

It could not have been because she was unsatisfied. Fuck no. I'd made sure she came at least twice for each of mine. Being a generous lover did not come naturally. I was more the conqueror type, but I could not get enough of her pleasure. In fact, her delightful whimpers and moans, the sultry way she said my name, the times she scored my back with her nails, it all only made the experience that much better.

We were combustible together, and I was dying to have another go. That kind of explosive passion was not easily attained. Even Marat had spoken of the lack of spark in his many encounters, and he had a plethora of lovers. I preferred to be alone, resigned to the fact I would die that way, while Marat fucked anything with a pussy, trying to fill the void within himself.

To each his own. I waited for the elevator to stop with no hint on my face that I was losing patience. Impatient men did not become billionaires. It had taken a long time to go from the streets of Moscow to the penthouses and top floors of Manhattan, but that was where we lived now.

"I will see you later," Marat said, walking to his office.

The morning was a never ending series of conference calls and looking over proposals. Multitasking was a rare talent for most men, but that was the thing about being a hunter. You needed to be able to concentrate on more than one thing at a time. So, while our attorneys arrived with important documents that needed signing around ten, I paid attention to them while my mind churned, thinking about her and what she'd been doing since she left the warmth of my bed, my penthouse, hell, maybe even the entire city, in the wee hours of the morning.

Did she have a car parked somewhere? Or did she take a cab or the subway? Where had she gone? Did she get there okay?

I wished she'd stayed. Wanted the pleasure of waking up with her in my arms. So soft. So warm. So breathtakingly delicious. Fuck, just remembering the taste of her made my cock thump behind my trousers. I ran a hand over my face. This was not like me. I hardly remembered the women I'd bedded in the past.

The second they left my bedroom, that was it. They were gone. Unimportant. Useful at the time. But nothing special. Just something to pass the time or scratch an itch. This woman was their opposite. She was special. And she was taking up way too much space in my head. I needed her found. What I'd told Marat in passing seemed like an ideal plan now.

I wanted to see her again, yes. But what I needed was to fuck her out of my system. Then I would be myself again. The wolf. The hunter. Not an animal made weak by desire, caught in her trap. No. I would never be that man. Anger rose inside me, but whether it was directed at her or myself, I could not be sure.

By the time our attorneys left, it was well into the

afternoon. I had skipped lunch, but I was not in the mood for food. It was something I hated doing, but I found it necessary on days like these. Going hungry by choice was a lot different from when we were children and there were no other options.

"Boss?"

Andres, my assistant, came into my office after the lawyers were packed up and gone. I'd head-hunted the younger man from a former competitor who I later bought out. That was some ten years ago now. I'd been unable to purchase or glean information from him using other, less savory means regarding the deal we were trying to make.

Afterwards, I offered Andres a job. Marat thought I was being sentimental, but I admired his loyalty and grit. Asking him to join our team was one of the best business decisions I had made. The man was like a walking, talking computer. He had a knack for recalling details with unerring accuracy, and I knew I could trust him with corporate secrets.

It took a few hours going over notes before we switched to the daily correspondence. Going through my email with Andres was always easier since he was better on the computer than I was. I did not have the patience for technology, ironic as that was. The metals we mined were necessary to keep such tech working, but I did not care which iPhone was out or what new gadget was the next best thing.

Facing the window, I watched the storm clouds gather among the skyscrapers and towers. Those mile high representations of humankind's genius stood in defiance of nature. Imagine that kind of brilliance to master physics, making history and erecting monuments that point directly at the heavens as if daring the gods to strike them down.

I admired the men and women who created such things. They must have had balls of steel to challenge the very beings responsible for creation itself. Like recalcitrant children asking their parents for a duel. Innovators were often mad, wasn't that a saying? I was sure I had heard it somewhere. I listened as Andres rattled off the rest of my schedule with about half the attention I should have given it.

"Dinner tonight at Chez Luis with Marcus Porter from Capital One at seven," he said.

"No. Move the dinner appointment to Marat's calendar. In fact, move all of them to my brother's schedule. I will be unavailable for everything save my office hours during the next few weeks."

"What about the Castle Ball on the twentieth? He will expect you to attend in person," Andres said.

"Fine, but make sure Marat and Josef, and you

too, Andres, make sure all three of you are on the list as well," I said, steepling my fingers as I continued to watch the storm clouds gathering.

"Very well, Mr. Volkov," he replied, frowning as he added the note.

Josef knocked and entered my office without waiting for a response. I ignored him while I rattled off replies to the most important of my messages. Andres typed everything into his tablet faster than a fifteen year old on TikTok.

Once we were finished, I turned my head and acknowledged Josef. It was after four now, and my business day was just getting started. He spoke into the mic hidden in his cuff link and pressed the com in his ear as he listened to whoever was speaking to him. He had come into our lives later, but if I had to choose anyone in the world other than Marat to guard my life, or the life of someone I care about, it would be him.

"What is it, Josef?" I asked, stepping inside my office, where Andres waited for me.

"We might have a line on the woman."

"Might?"

"Yes. I think you will appreciate this. She arrived at the party last night as Missy Castle's plus one."

"Missy Castle?"

"Indeed. She's Matthew Castle's sister. If my information is correct, I know your mystery woman's name."

"Well. What is it?" I growled, impatient.

"Sofia DiFalco. She works as Missy Castle's personal assistant, but I understand she is an aspiring novelist."

"A novelist?"

That was surprising. I never met a novelist, not even an aspiring one. My heart hammered inside my chest at the prospect of seeing her, *Sofia DiFalco*, again. I trusted Josef to have already put together a dossier on the woman, and I stood from my desk, hand out for the tablet Andres held. He gave it to me immediately.

"Send me everything you found and get the car," I instructed.

"Yes, boss."

"Where is she now?"

"She rents a shitty apartment in a Midtown."

I grunted and scrolled to the file, opening it as I walked to the elevator. Josef had already called for the car and was seeing to security as I read more about the woman who rocked my world last night.

Sofia. I liked the sound of her name. The more I played it over and over again in my mind the better it sounded. She was almost ten years my junior. She'd turned twenty-eight years old this past November, and I frowned, wondering if she would mind the age difference. She did not seem to mind it last night, but what did it matter, anyway?

I was not proposing marriage. Just a short arrangement. A month. That was it. A month to fuck her out of my system and get my brain focused back on what was important. Business. Family. That was all I had room for in my life. But even billionaire bosses deserved a vacation once in a while.

Sofia DiFalco was mine.

I got canned. I couldn't fucking believe it.

Brown water poured from the spout, and I hustled to turn it off before it could fill the tub. Dammit. I really wanted a bath. I rubbed my hands together, trying to get my circulation going. Despite the two pairs of pants, a long-sleeved thermal shirt, and an enormous, hooded sweatshirt on top of that depicting a grumpy faced cat, I was still freezing.

"Fuck this day, already," I growled, my potty mouth getting the better of me as usual.

It was bad enough I had to fork out seventy-three dollars for an Uber that morning, which made my walk of shame not only embarrassing but detrimental to my budget, but when I got home, my boss called. She sounded frantic, which was not unusual, and angry, which was.

"Sofia! Why didn't you answer my calls on your cell?"

"Hello, Missy. Um, because my cell died. Why? What's wrong?"

Typically, my week was Monday through Friday. Weekends were my own since Missy often spent them at her family home in the Hamptons during the summer and the Long Island Sound during the winter months. She and her brother were an odd pair. I never really liked being around him and was grateful it hadn't happened very often. If Missy was flighty, then Matthew was straight up creepy.

So I was grateful for the fact Missy usually reserved time with her brother for the weekends at one of their estates. And that was when I worked on my book and visited my family. I only worked if she really needed me, and last night she insisted I go to the party but gave no indication she needed me after. I had no idea what she was talking about when she called to fire me.

"I can't believe it. How could you do this to me?"

"Missy, I have no idea what you're talking about."

I'd replied to her hysterics with an eye roll. She was pretty much the worst drama queen I knew. Something that was definitely going in my book.

"Matthew is just livid. Now, he's talking about cutting off my allowance. I'm sorry, Sof."

"Sorry for what, Missy. What are you saying?" I asked, completely bewildered.

"I just can't have you work for me anymore."

She hadn't made much sense, but then again, she rarely did. Coming from one of the wealthiest families on the East Coast, I'd imagined that was a rich people problem. But the reality was she fired me.

I understood that quite clearly. She'd uttered something about loyalty and the bonds of womanhood or some such thing, then she hung up. To say I was put out would be mild. Truth was, I was pissed.

I didn't know what bonds of womanhood I had destroyed, but if I was fired, then that meant I needed a new job, and soon. I walked over to the radiator, testing it with my hands. Nope. Still cold, despite Mr. Crawford, my landlord, insisting he fixed the issue with the heat.

I grabbed a wooden spoon and started banging on the cold hunk of metal, cursing it out while I did. Maybe that was why I hadn't heard anyone knocking on the door. At least, not until they came crashing through it.

"Aghhh!"

"Zaika, are you okay?"

I clapped my hands over my mouth as six and a half feet of furious Russian came racing towards me. His hands dragged me towards him, and he ran them over my lumpy ensemble as if checking me for breaks and fractures. I stood stone still for a moment until sanity returned. Then I slapped at his fingers, and backed up as far as I could, which was all of two feet before the wall stopped me.

"I'm fine! Oh my God, what are you doing here?"

My cheeks were burning, and I could only imagine what I looked like. He dragged his gaze up my body and when it finally met mine—*bam*. I felt it hit me with all the force of a Mack truck. Attraction sizzled between us, and I had to wonder if maybe I wasn't hallucinating.

"Boss, is she okay?" a large man wielding a gun asked, and I screamed.

"She is fine. Sofia, this man is my head of security. Why were you banging that spoon?" he asked, dismissing my little freak out.

"What? Oh! Nothing, I was just trying to make the radiator work. But how did you find out where I lived? And who told you my name?"

I was panicking, but who could blame me? There were now four gigantic men stalking around my two by four apartment, walking on my broken linoleum floor with their expensive Italian shoes. I closed my eyes, counting to three. Maybe when I opened them this would all be some cold-induced hallucination?

One. Two. Three. Nope.

He was still there, head canted to the side like a wild animal as he observed my mini melt down. Did he have to be so big? I was short, but I was not a small woman. Still, he made me feel positively petite. I'd had a chance to Google him when I got home, and what I found made my hands tremble as he stood there, taking up all the available space in the room.

Adrik Volkov wasn't some relative of whoever owned Volkov Industries. He was not some rich guy with a common Russian surname. He was the motherfucking head of Volkov Industries. Rumored to be associated with illegal activities—the guy was a former fucking crime lord, for fuck's sake!

"Leave us," he commanded, affording one glance at the head giant who mumbled something into his suit cuff.

My entire body was on high alert, and I hated to admit it, but something happened to me when he barked out commands like that. Something I would deny if asked. I tried to slow my pulse, but nothing could stop my sex from clenching and moisture from pooling between my thighs. Seconds later, the men who'd been scurrying through my apartment high-tailed it out of there. They were well-trained, I'd give them that. But still, scary as fuck. I could breathe a little easier without them, but only by a smidgeon.

Adrik watched with a hawk-like focus that made me feel like a bug in a display case. I was stunned. Had no idea what he was doing there or why he had bothered hunting me down. Did he have some sort of spyware that told him when people searched his name on the internet? No. That was dumb. Mostly. Honestly, I didn't know what he was capable of, but if the rumors were true, it was a lot.

Gulp.

He stood and stared at me, as if waiting for something. But what was I supposed to say to him? I had questions, but none I was secure enough to voice aloud. And definitely not to him. The seconds ticked by slow as hours and I had no idea how long we stood like that, just facing off. I inhaled a deep breath.

"Your face is very revealing, Zaika moya," he whispered, but I remained quiet.

What could I say, really? I'd never been in a situation like that before. I tried to look unaffected, you know, cool and calm, but I imagined I looked like a crazy person. My getup was downright hilarious next to his fancy suit, but it wasn't like I'd been expecting company.

"You are thinking something, Zaika. Tell me."

So, were mind blowing, pussy breaking one night stands supposed to track you down the next day at your apartment and just sorta pop up unannounced for shits and giggles?

But I wasn't saying all that to him. I mean, who would?

"Pussy breaking? I promise, Zaika moya, if I did this terrible thing, I will fix it," he whispered, eyes darkening as they raked over my body again.

"Shit. I said that out loud, didn't I? Um, tea?" I asked, my voice unnaturally high-pitched.

"I drink tea," he said, following me into my postage stamp sized kitchen.

I pressed the button for the electric kettle and got down two mugs, furiously wiping the one with the impossible to remove coffee stain. He stopped my scrubbing with one big hand on my wrist. I didn't turn to face him. I couldn't, at least, not until my body stopped trembling. He smelled so good. Spicy and expensive. Heat seemed to radiate from him, and in my now frigid apartment, I could not help but move closer, seeking his warmth.

"The cup is clean, Zaika," he whispered, and his breath tickled my cheek. "Don't tell me you are nervous after everything we did last night?"

I closed my eyes again at the feel of his warm body almost touching mine, but not quite. The tease. His cologne was something I did not recognize as being anything other than him. It was exotic, unusual, like spice and man and something wild and dangerous.

"Maybe that is why I'm nervous. What are you doing here?" I asked, finally finding the courage to meet his steely gaze.

"I-I have a proposal for you," he said, but it sounded like he was going to say something else first.

Despite being all but frozen a second ago, I was suddenly sweating like crazy. My heart pounded, and a sizzle of excitement spiked up my spin. A proposal? Was this guy nuts?

"Look, last night was fun and all, but I don't go around marrying strangers no matter how sexy they are," I began.

Adrik cocked his head to the side again, eyes flashing with some intense emotion. I couldn't tell if it was anger, surprise, lust, or maybe repulsion. Then he smirked, and my panties just up and melted. Holy. Shit. No one man should embody that much sex appeal. It just wasn't fair to the rest of the poor schleps out there trying to get by.

"I am glad you find me sexy, Zaika. But this is not my proposal."

"What?" I asked dumbly.

"I was not asking you to marry me, Sofia. Nothing so rash as this," he began.

"Oh, good," I said.

I forced a laugh, turning around so I could grab tea bags from the ceramic cat jar I kept on the counter. I was really trying to hide my embarrassment. Of course, this man wasn't proposing to me. Me? Of all people. He was Adrik fucking Volkov. He probably had some model thin Russian bride waiting for him in Siberia or some shit. What did he need with a chubby, loudmouthed American?

"I am not the marrying kind, you understand? So, I want you to move in with me for the next month," he announced, just dropping that bomb on me like— *boom!*

"What?!" I screeched, dropping both mugs in my hand with two loud, messy crashes.

Tea and glass went everywhere, and Adrik cursed

roundly in Russian. For a moment, I thought he was upset because I'd splashed tea on his expensive pants, then he grabbed my waist and lifted me up, sitting my stunned ass on my counter while he scrounged under the sink for some dish towels to drop on the mess.

"You must be more careful, Zaika moya. No shoes on your feet. You could be hurt," he growled, mopping up the mess with more efficiency than I would have given a man in his position credit for.

"Sorry," I mumbled, still too shocked to form sentences. "Did you say you want me to move in with you for a month?"

"Yes. I am a very busy man, but I am practical. I have needs, but I am in the middle of a very important negotiation. I can't afford to spend time wooing you. Now, I happen to know you are suddenly without employment," he said, straightening up and dropping the whole mess into the trash can, towels and all.

"I liked that daisy towel," I muttered.

He ignored that and continued to explain his reasoning to me. I supposed I should have been flattered. But I was too shocked to appreciate the situation.

"Just like I know you are writing a novel and

could use someone who has the power to whisper in the ear of the right publishing house. My proposal is you stay with me for one month, all expenses paid, including your rent, utilities, and heat," he said, looking around dubiously. "Plus, you will have an unlimited platinum card for shopping, clothes, nails, hair whatever you want. At the end of the month, my people will arrange a meeting for you with whichever publisher you choose."

My brain was spinning. He was like a damn devil, offering me what I wanted most of all in return for my body—or was it my soul he was really after? Of all the arrogant, half-assed—wait, what did he say? This guy knew publishers, too? That was it, the last straw that broke this fluffy camel's back.

"Out," I growled.

"Pardon?" he asked.

I could tell by his apparent confusion he really did not understand what was happening. So I slid off the counter where he'd placed me like I weighed next to nothing, and I pointed to the door, stomping my foot, which had no effect considering I wore socks and no shoes.

"I said get out."

"Zaika—"

"My name is Sofia, as you somehow found out—

creepy, by the way. And I don't need your help whispering into anyone's ears, got it? I don't care who you know. I will publish my book based on the merits of my writing or not at all!"

Adrik looked at me, a mixture of admiration and exasperation on his face. It was the look you gave a spoiled child, or someone who did not know any better, and I found it completely demeaning.

How dare he?

"You are an innocent, Zaika moya. That is why you do not understand, it is always about who you know," he said slowly, as if I was too dim to get what he meant.

Ooooh. That made my blood boil. And not in the happy times fun way that had occurred between us the previous night. An image of the reflection I'd seen of myself, legs on his shoulders as he ate my pussy like a starving man, in one of the ceiling to floor windows of his penthouse flashed inside my brain, and I wobbled a little on my feet. Then I narrowed my eyes at him. Why deny what happened?

"Considering I was riding your face last night like a rodeo cowgirl, I don't think I'm all that innocent. So, fuck you very much for that indecent proposal. You can leave now."

"But that's just it. I can't leave," he growled angrily, and no, he did not look happy about it.

Wasn't that too bad? I was pissed as well. So much so, I was vibrating with it. Smug bastard. Did he think this was *Pretty Woman*? Did I look like Julia fucking Roberts? For a moment, I'd actually thought he was proposing to me, when really, he was proposing I be his whore for a month.

I didn't know why I was so disappointed. I didn't expect the man had fallen in love with me overnight. Yeah, I mean, he looked a little nuts hunting me down the next day, but that was probably because rich men were used to getting their way. Maybe I should have been flattered. Maybe later, I would be. But I was too angry and confused, and cold to think straight.

Did he have to look so good in his exquisitely tailored coat and suit? Even cursing and pulling on his thick dark hair, he was sexy as sin. I looked down at my furry sock covered feet and closed my eyes. Him proposing to me? I must have been suffering from a senior moment to think something like that.

But really, what the heck was he thinking, finding my address, and coming here to proposition me? Poor billionaire. He'd been duped. Last night I had been in costume. Not anymore, though. Sweatpants and hoodies were my usual weekend attire. He needed someone who wore silk stockings and stilettos. That was not me. It never would be. And if I'd given him the impression I was for sale, I guess maybe I was to blame, too.

"Look, I am sorry to interrupt your tirade, but I really don't know what to tell you, Adrik. I am not a prostitute. But I am sure someone with your connections can find one. I mean, you look like you can definitely afford to buy anyone you want. Except me. Now, goodbye," I said stiffly.

"No."

He shook his head, looking like a beast instead of a man as he stalked from wall to wall, wearing a path across the old carpet with his expensive shoes.

"No?"

"Yes."

"Yes?"

Adrik expelled a breath and stopped his pacing to answer me.

"Yes, to the first *no*. No. That is my answer to your rebuttal. You do not understand, I don't want anyone else. I want you. Now, I have already bought this building. If you refuse me, I will take over all the apartments. You and your neighbors will have nowhere to go—"

"Then I will go home, I have family, you know. And shame on you for threatening to put poor people on the streets," I said, furious he would even suggest such a thing.

"I would do worse things than that, Zaika. I have done. And yes, let us talk about your family. Your father is unemployable. Alcoholic, yes?"

"Don't talk about my father! He's had some problems, but he's doing his best and Nonna—"

"We shall agree to disagree about what means his best. As for your grandmother. She is a good woman, responsible. She cared for you, yes?"

"She raised me," I whispered, hating where this was going.

"Yes. Like I said. Good woman. But also deeply in debt. The rest of your family can barely get by. But they all live together. Nice family. Loving. Unfortunately, the mortgage is past due, and the property taxes have been unpaid for six months."

"W-what?" I asked, sitting down hard.

It bothered me that he brought up my father, but he was not saying anything that wasn't true. Dad was an alcoholic. His broken heart after my mother died allowed for nothing else. There was no room for anything but grief. Certainly not me.

But all that was in the past. I forgave my father

for his sins long ago. What I did not know was that Grandma was so far behind. Fear filled me and worry, too. My grandmother had paid for my college. Helping me when my father was incapable. I always swore to pay her back someday.

"But do not worry, Zaika moya. I bought the lien on this property in North Bergen right before we got here. I now hold the mortgage on it."

"Y-you did that in case I said no to your crazy and insulting plan to have me be your whore?" I asked, eyes so wide I wondered if it was possible for them to pop right out of my head.

"No, Zaika. Not my whore. Just mine. For one month. I wanted to make sure you understand how valuable this one month is to me."

I could not believe this man. He'd dug into my life, violating me in ways I had never experienced. And what for? To have me as his beck and call fuck buddy? It shouldn't have stroked my ego that he thought I was good in the sack, but it did. Good enough to warrant him going through all this trouble just to fuck me again. But I couldn't help it.

Yep. There was something definitely wrong with me. That I would even consider being flattered by this monster. But even as I thought the word, I couldn't help the quiver rolling through me. My body swelled and clenched at the remembered passion between us. That much was undeniable. Adrik and I were fire when we touched.

"Your phone is ringing, Zaika. Take the call."

My body moved automatically to obey his rough command, but it was too late to stop. My grandmother's name flashed across my cell phone, and I answered it immediately.

"Nonna? Wait, slow down. The bank called? Uncle Frank? No! Do not give him power of attorney, Nonna. I will be there in one hour. Promise me you won't do anything. Just promise! Okay, yeah, I am on my way."

My heart was beating me to death, but not because of the figure he cut in his tailored suit or because of how out of place he looked in my crappy apartment. Uncle Frank was a prick, and whatever manipulations Adrik set into motion to get me to agree to his cockamamie plan, he obviously hadn't dug deep enough into my family to know about my father's sister's husband. A man I hated more than any other on the planet. A look of confusion crossed Adrik's face, and he flashed a glare at one of his henchmen.

"On it," the man murmured, already on his phone.

"Come. My car is outside."

I put my ugly, puffy winter coat on, and my over-socked feet shoved inside a pair of scuffed-up boots, not giving two shits what I looked like. Grabbing my backpack, which doubled as a purse, I shoved my wallet inside, knowing my tablet and other crap were already in it.

Adrik's men held the door of his sleek limousine open for us and I slid inside, too incensed to do much but get in. I had to get Uncle Frank out of there before that sleazeball did something that couldn't be undone. I'd stopped the fucker once, but I didn't know if I could live with myself if he took Nonna's building from her.

"We will be there in forty-one minutes. Less if Carlo speeds, and he will. Now, tell me what I need to know about this Uncle Frank."

I turned my head and looked into Adrik's impossibly dark eyes. A minute ago, this man was my enemy, and I really should not look at him like he was a savior. But if he could help my grandmother, whom I owed everything to, then I would just have to trust him.

CHAPTER FIVE
ADRIK

North Bergen was like most Jersey towns, only this one seemed to be designed by a lunatic. Whoever planned that city must have been fucked up on something strong, because the streets made no sense. Never mind that some were so steep they were on seventy degree angles, but others just stopped in the middle of the map with no rhyme or reason.

I could not imagine learning to drive in such a town or riding a bicycle. But this was where Sofia had grown up. I frowned as we sat in the heavy traffic, even more dense in Jersey than it was in Manhattan. But eventually, and under the original forty-one minute timeline, we arrived.

I put my hand on Sofia's thigh, stopping her from

jumping out of the vehicle before my guy could open the door. She looked down but did not remove it, and something spiked within my blood. Pride maybe that she obeyed, that she trusted me to keep her safe.

Imagine that? A soft bunny who trusted her safety to the hungry wolf who stalked her. I cocked my head to the side, memorizing the feel of her through the layers of cheap clothes she wore. Not that it mattered to me. I liked her better naked, anyway.

During the ride, Sofia told me about this Uncle Frank. Her paternal Aunt Linda's husband was a real winner. Not. Josef sent me a file on him ten minutes after we left her apartment and I'd glanced over it while she spoke. Frank Russo was a sonovabitch plain and simple. A low level wannabe mafioso who liked to gamble and fuck hookers. Young hookers.

I did not miss the revulsion in her eyes when Sofia spoke of the man. She was hiding something from me, and I had my own idea just what Uncle Frank had been like when Sofia was younger. The thought filled me with rage. I released my hold as Josef opened the door, checking traffic to make sure we could cross the busy street unscathed. The winter wind was bitter, and I scowled at the slushy, unkempt sidewalk outside of her grandmother's building.

"Shit. Dad is supposed to shovel," she mumbled.

The abject misery on her face tugged at something inside me—*could it be my heart?* I was not sure. It had been a long time since I felt anything like that.

"Nonna? Dad?" Sofia called as we walked inside past the front door with the broken lock.

The building was five levels, ten units, including a finished basement. Her grandmother owned the building, and all the apartments were supposedly rented to Sofia's family members. But from what I could tell, the old woman was lenient, and her family took advantage. That was why the taxes were not paid and liens were heavy on the property. My people had even discovered a second mortgage, which had been taken out in Sofia's father's name.

I did not know yet if it was really him who took the money, but I would find out. Eventually. I flashed my gaze to Josef, and mind reader that he was, he nodded. I wanted the street cleaned, the front door more secure. And I wanted help for her father. But this was nothing I needed to worry Sofia's pretty head about. She would not like my interference, but some things were a nonnegotiable part of my nature. I was not a saint. Never claimed to be.

There was arguing coming from inside the first floor apartment, as well as a wonderful smell. Someone was cooking, and the aroma was divine. My men sniffed loudly, and my own stomach growled. Fuck. That was why I hated skipping meals. Sofia looked at me over her shoulder, frowning as she pulled open the door.

"Nonna, I'm here. Frank, you stop right there!" Sofia yelled.

She pointed at a man in a velour track suit who was pushing a pen towards an older woman, her grandmother I guessed, as he stood menacingly over her. There was a younger female, mid-forties, sitting at the table. She looked haggard and dazed, clearly on something, as she smoked her e-cigarette and scrolled through her phone. She hadn't even looked up when we walked in. The man, though. He noticed. His eyes bugged out of his head as I walked in behind Sofia with three heavily armed men and Josef.

"Sofia!" The older woman cried out and stood up to grab Sofia in a fierce hug.

"Nonna," Sofia said, catching the old woman's

face in her hands and kissing each of her rosy cheeks.

I watched silently at the byplay, a sense of pride and approval filling me as I watched her put her grandmother at ease. She squared off with this uncle who shrugged and pretended to be the good guy.

"Sof, baby, you know I just wanna help Nonna out. I've been telling her this place is too, uh, big for her, but Uncle Frank can take care of it. Now, come on. Don't be so angry. You know me, kiddo," he said, and grinned at her.

I did not like the look on his face. It was not how an uncle should look at his niece. I stepped forward, getting right into the man's face.

"Sofia? Who are these men?" Nonna asked.

"Oh, um, Nonna, everyone, this is Adrik, he's m-my," she stuttered, warm brown eyes flashing to me.

"Adrik Volkov," I said, turning away from the foul smelling man to shake the old woman's hand.

"Volkov? Hmm, I know this name," Nonna said, pulling me into a hug with surprising strength. "Call me Nonna. And you are?" she asked, turning to Josef next.

I was stunned. Shocked that this tiny grand-mother had not only pulled me and all four of my guards into a hug, but she was now scooping bowls of homemade pasta out and pushing them at us, insisting we sit down to eat.

"Uh, thank you, Nonna," I said, while Sofia smirked at me from across the room.

"You know, Sof. We don't need outsiders here while we talk family business."

Uncle Frank walked across the eat-in kitchen and turned his back, like he was trying to cut me out of the conversation. The man did not know who he was dealing with. While my men sat down, bullied by an old woman, I joined Sofia and Frank on the other side of the room.

"I don't know what you're playing at, but you will never get this building," Sofia hissed.

"Don't say never, baby girl," he whispered, and before I knew it I had him by the back of the neck.

Frank squeaked as I clapped his shoulder with my free hand, pretending a joviality I was not feeling in the slightest. The woman, who I assumed was Frank's wife, still did not look up. She paid us no mind, and Nonna was busy grating cheese over what smelled like a perfectly made plate of homemade cavatelli for Josef who was just smiling like the cat that ate the canary.

Lucky bastard. I was starving. But I needed to take care of this first.

"She is not your baby girl, Frank. And this building is not yours. Like she said, It never will be," I whispered in his ear.

"Hey, what do you know? The old lady can't afford it and I got friends," he whined.

"Your friends know who I am, Frank. Ask them about Adrik Volkov. Ask them about the Dark Wolf," I told him.

I looked at Sofia, watching her as she watched me handle this piece of shit man. She did not look frightened. In fact, she looked content to see me terrorize him. Good. I would do that for her and more. Gladly. I let go of Frank's neck, and he almost fell to the floor.

"Leave. Now."

He nodded, scrambling to his feet as he grabbed his wife's arm and pulled her along with him, barely taking the time to say goodbye. Nonna did not seem to mind. She was still coddling my men, and I growled, sending them all into a frenzy. They ate quickly and cleaned up, then left the room without me having to tell them.

"Oh, Sofia, I am so glad you came. After the bank called to tell me the liens and mortgage were bought, I was so confused. Then Uncle Frank came over and you know he tries this with me almost daily now," she said, wringing her hands.

"It's okay, Nonna. Everything is going to be okay," she said, hugging the old woman to her chest.

I stilled, watching Sofia's face as she lifted her gaze to mine and mouthed the one word I wanted to hear since I found her.

Yes.

My heart started pounding, but I made no outward sign of what was happening inside me. No. I would not have allowed Frank to take advantage of the old woman who'd fed me and my men. I was still coming out of the carb coma her pasta had put me under, and stood up to clean my place while Sofia spoke in hushed tones to her grandmother.

The kitchen had standard oak cabinets and stainless steel sink. Weathered wall paper in patterns of beige and yellow lined the walls. It was clean, but old, and well-used. I washed my dish and put it in the sink. Searching for a towel to dry my hands when one was pushed at me.

"Well, how do we do this?" Sofia asked, and I raised my eyebrows as I patted my hands dry.

"You knew well enough how to do it last night, *Zaika moya*," I replied, my mind going right to the gutter.

"I don't mean that," she said, and her cheeks turned a dusky shade of rose. "I mean, what are the terms exactly?"

"The terms? It is simple. You live with me for one month, expenses paid and compensation will be granted."

"The lien will be forgiven, and the mortgage brought current?" she asked.

No. I would pay everything off, hire a manager to set the rest of the family right, and fix some of the much needed repairs that even I could see. But she did not need those details. So, I nodded my head.

"And Uncle Frank won't get his hands on the property?"

"Never, Zaika," I promised.

Uncle Frank was going to be far too busy running from me to worry about trying to swindle his mother-in-law out of her property. Sofia did not realize she had the wolf in her corner now. She was safe. So was everyone she loved.

But it is only for a month, I reminded myself. Yes. One month. And I was going to enjoy every second of it. I was going to burn through this desire I felt for her, and when it was over, I would still be standing. I did not fully understand my obsession with this woman, but at least I had the chance to cure my fixation.

That was the plan. Keep fucking my Zaika until I no longer felt this ravaging hunger inside my blood.

"What about the rules? Between us for the next month. What is it you want?"

"What do you mean? You will live with me for the next month. You will belong to me. And I will have you, Zaika moya. I plan to fuck you every way I can in that time," I growl, sounding more like an animal than a man.

But that was how obsessed I was with this woman. She drove me wild. Made me want and hunger in ways I had not felt since maybe ever. Not even when I was a teenager did I get this hard thinking about a woman. My cock jerked, precum leaking from my slit, making my boxers damp.

"Um, I don't think I like anal," she stated, and my eyebrows raised.

"You have tried anal?" I asked.

Fuck, my balls seized up, my dick readier than ever to test that theory. Yes, I would have her in every way. Her mouth. Her tits. Her ass. That sweet pussy of hers. My dirty little Zaika would beg for my dick to fill every one of her holes before the month was over.

"Not exactly," she mumbled, and her cheeks grew even redder.

"Then how do you know?" I asked.

"I don't know, it's just, I don't like pain."

"I promise you, Zaika, everything we do together will be mutually pleasurable or not done at all."

"Okay," she replied, exhaling slowly.

"Anything else?" I asked, curious to hear what would come out of her mouth next.

"Are you gonna—that is, will there be other women, or men, during this month?"

"You will have no one but me, understood?"

"That's a double standard," she mumbled, but I was not amused.

I grabbed her chin with my forefinger and thumb and turned her face up towards me.

"I was not finished. For the next month, you belong to me. I do not share what is mine. No one else will touch this skin, look at this flesh, or hear those soft desperate noises you make. No one but me."

She swallowed and her eyes darkened, the warm brown turning to molten chocolate as my words met her ears. I was not immune to that look on her face, and my pants tightened as my cock grew hard just thinking of the way she had looked last night, spread eagle, bare, glistening, quivering eagerly for my touch.

"And you? Other women?"

I straightened my shoulders, my obsidian stare raking across her skin as I tilted my head arrogantly. I'd been called good looking before, but I never gave it much thought till then. But I appreciated it as I stared at Zaika Mona and her mutinous expression.

A smile tugged at the corner of my lips, but I refused to give in. She looked like she wanted to stomp her feet or slap me, demanding an answer with a fiery gleam in her eye. I could make an ass of myself, or I could toy with her. But I did neither. I tugged on my lower lip, possessive madness holding me in its grips, and I replied truthfully.

"I told you, Zaika moya. I only want you."

CHAPTER SIX
SOFIA

After accepting Adrik's proposal, everything seemed to happen in a rush. We spent a few more minutes visiting with Nonna as if I hadn't just accepted a very naughty proposition from the most powerful man I had ever met inside the kitchen where I used to bake cookies as a child. I ran to the upstairs apartment where my father still lived, and kissed his cheek while he slept, keeled over in front of the television.

A half-empty bottle of scotch sat on the floor at his feet, and tears welled in my eyes when I saw it. But I didn't have the heart to pour it down the drain. His illness was too far gone for such tactics to work. He needed professional help, but asking for it was step one. Far as I knew, Dad didn't want to get better. I left soon after I entered, stopping to kiss Nonna one more time.

The ride back to the city was fast, at least it seemed that way. Adrik was on his phone for most of it, and I huffed more than one long breath. What was all the urgency if he was just going to ignore me? Granted, the million plus dollars he'd spent gobbling up properties that had anything to do with me were likely a drop in the bucket for him. But still. A girl had to wonder.

All the excitement and absurdity of the day must have caught up to me, and I fell asleep. I only knew that because when I woke up, I was floating. Well, not really floating, but being carried in a pair of strong, muscular arms.

"Easy, Zaika moya. I got you."

That was what had me worried. He did have me. And the fact he was not even out of breath while he carried my fluffy butt the entire elevator ride and then through his penthouse until we reached his bedroom had my attention. Adrik was stronger than he looked. Or maybe not. Because honestly, who looked like him? Besides professional athletes and maybe the guy who played that Viking king's brother, but that was it. There couldn't be that many enormous, not to mention gorgeous, billionaires running around Manhattan. At least, not as far as I knew.

He placed me on his bed, stepping back as if I'd burned him. I sat up, clearing my throat. This was so fucked up. I was fucked up. I wanted to be indignant and angry, but the truth was, I also wanted him to want me. And I was hurt that he was standing there stoically and not pouncing.

"Sorry, uh, I guess it all caught up to me," I said.

"Yes. I imagine it did. Would you like a drink?" he offered, raising one perfect eyebrow.

Christ, he is so handsome.

His features could have been chiseled from marble. His hair was combed back, thick, and glossy. He had one of those permanent five o'clock shadow beards, and I had to admit, I couldn't think of anything sexier than a man with some scruff on his cheeks.

Adrik oozed sex and, sex fiend that I was surely becoming, I wanted to lick every inch of him from head to toe.

"Um, sure. I'd like a drink."

That was an understatement. I waited as he poured two fingers of scotch into a crystal glass and handed it to me. Sipping too quickly, I gasped and sputtered, using the back of my hand to wipe the fiery amber liquid that I managed to dribble like a baby down my chin.

"Small sips, Zaika."

"Now you tell me," I mumbled.

Forcing myself to stand, I placed the glass on the dresser. His bedroom loomed before me, done in grays and blacks. It was so utterly masculine. The same wolf that served as his company's logo, the one he had inked onto his back looked down at me from the ceiling where a mural had been painted.

Holy fuck. It was beautiful, menacing, but it filled me with a sense of peace. Like the wolf was watching over us, keeping us safe. That was ridiculous. I snapped my attention to the enormous windows and frowned.

"Can people see us in here?"

"No. The glass is special. No one can see inside, and depending on the setting, the light will filter through however little or much I desire."

"Wow. That is incredible," I said and meant it.

"So, this is your room, but where do I sleep?"

"Here, of course," he said, spreading his arms wide as if it were simple.

"No. You had your chance to talk terms, and you never said I had to sleep with you."

"Of course, I did—"

"No, you really didn't. I agreed to live with you and have sex with you for one month, Adrik. But I won't sleep beside you."

However, I'd expected him to react, what he did next was so not it. Adrik snarled something in Russian. It must have been a curse. But it wasn't the profanity that made me freeze like a deer in headlights. It was the sound he made. Like a motherfucking animal.

He stepped forward, barking commands at me in a language he knew I did not speak. As if he was too angry by the fact I'd outwitted him to remember English. Odd really because most of the time he didn't even have an accent. Only when his emotions ran high could I hear his Eastern European origins.

He grabbed the hem of my sweatshirt and pulled it over my head, spinning me around to face away from. Next, he took the waistband of both pairs of pants I had on and pushed them down. For some reason, I helped, kicking them off my legs, then cursing myself for my own stupid complicity.

The muted violence in his movements should have scared me. Christ knew I was breathing like I'd just taken a spin class. But instead of fear, my pussy throbbed and grew slick with need. The man was turning me on like no one else ever had.

I was speechless. No one had ever treated me that way. He fisted the collar of the oversized t-shirt I had on and ripped it right off my body. I'd foregone a bra since a) I wasn't planning to leave my apartment that day, and b) with all those layers, who needed one?

My panties were next, and then I felt him pushing his knee between my thighs as he bent me over the bed. I moaned when my nipples came into contact with the bedding, panting now that he was running his hands over my flesh.

"So fucking beautiful, Zaika," he growled, calling me that Russian pet name he seemed stuck on.

I'd have to remember to ask him what it meant once I was capable of speech. He tugged on my hips, positioning me so I was on my knees, thighs spread, ass in the air, face and chest pressed on the mattress. Again, the windows acted like mirrors and since his bedroom was in the corner, I could see our reflections either way I turned my head.

He tore off his own jacket and shirt, but that was all he managed before he leaned forward and pressed the flat of his tongue *there*. I moaned loudly. No one had ever done that to me before. Adrik growled, using his hands to spread me wide as he licked me from asshole to clit, his fingers seeking, searching, exploring both orifices and I could not do anything but feel. And feel I did. I moaned as he licked me, thrusting his fingers inside my pussy, then using those same arousal-coated digits to press inside my ass.

"You can't," I said, gasping on the words. But he could. And he did.

I expected pain, but that was not what happened. Oh, Adrik was feeling something. Anger. Outsmarted. Fierce desire. Maybe a need to dominate me. But here was the real kicker. I loved it. He was taking me to a place I'd never been, and I could not wait for him to raise the stakes.

As if on cue, I felt his teeth graze across my right ass cheek. Then he bit me. Hard.

"Ow!"

The bite was followed by kisses, then his tongue. He licked and soothed the sting with his mouth. So soft, so good. Christ, the man had talent. He was driving me insane, making me come undone with hardly any effort at all. I was completely at his mercy. And that was bad because I wasn't sure if he had any mercy in him.

I moaned, rocking against his hand, wanting him deeper. He grunted in approval, palming my ass cheek as if proud of the print he undoubtedly put there. Fuck. Just thinking about it made me even wetter.

"Please," I begged, trying to rock back against him.

"Shhh, Zaika. So needy," he whispered, the smug bastard smirking as he did.

Before I could scream at him to stop messing around, he went back to licking my clit, forcing me to lose my mind. But never letting me come. On and on, his sensual torture continued. He'd lick my clit, fucking me with his fingers in my ass, and my pussy, but then he'd stop and withdraw, slowing down so I couldn't achieve orgasm. And I really, really wanted to come.

Finally, the sound of him undoing his belt and the swoosh of fabric as his pants slid off his powerful legs, all the way to the floor reached my ears, and it was like music. One of his fingers was still inside my ass, and he was stroking me slowly, moving in circles that teased all my senses. I'd never had that there before. It was strange and new, dirty in a good way. If I said I missed it when he withdrew, that would be an understatement. I fucking moaned when he pulled out and the bastard chuckled again.

"Forward, Zaika," he growled, slapping my ass

cheek gently, and I crawled up the bed, making room for him.

I was so damn eager for his possession I was dripping with it. I gasped when the mattress dipped, adjusting to his weight as he joined me. His large, calloused hands felt good against my soft skin as he ran them over my back and shoulders, my ass, my pussy, and my thighs. I moaned and leaned back, but he held me firm, as if this was part of the ritual of lovemaking. His hands moved around to my belly, my breasts, and throat. All the while, he whispered to me in a husky voice, words I did not understand.

By the time I heard him rip open the packet and slide the condom on his cock, I was almost there. Adrik kneeled behind me, hands on my hips as he pulled me back so his cock was lined up with my slit.

"Now, the month begins. Right now, Zaika. Here. With me buried inside your sweet pussy."

Then he slammed into me. Deep, hard, eliciting a guttural moan from my lips.

"Now, our real terms. You live here for one month," he grunted, pulling out almost all the way and staying there until his next words. "I fuck you when I say. Where I say."

Slam.

He filled me again, and I gasped. Adrik's hand

snaked around my hip, and he started pressing his thumb against my swollen clit. His cock jerked inside me, and my sheath tightened around him. It almost hurt when he pulled out this time, just leaving the tip inside.

"This bed is your bed. You will sleep here," he growled, slamming into me again in one hard thrust.

His hips were flush against my ass, and I didn't know how long I could take it. His cock was so thick, so long, it stretched and burned so good. I was so close. I wanted to move, needed to move, but his heavy weight held me down. I was powerless against him, pressed between the rock hard wall of his chest and the mattress.

"You belong to me now, Zaika," he growled in my ear.

"For one month," I answered, unable to help myself.

He froze, and I wanted to whimper, but managed to hold the sound deep within. There was something dangerous about hm. Something dangerous about me if I was willing to risk the former criminal, now powerful billionaire's wrath. But I wouldn't hold my tongue for anyone. Not even him.

"Da. One month. Starting now," he grunted,

holding my arms behind me as he started pounding into me at a relentless pace.

Tears pricked my eyes, but I wasn't in pain. On the contrary, there was something about being pinned by him, held in this position that was so damn comforting. Like I could just let go of everything. All the responsibility. All the baggage. I could simply toss it onto his capable shoulders and let him carry it awhile. As long as he didn't stop fucking me.

"I won't, Zaika. I will not stop fucking you. Now, come."

The command from his lips was the push I needed, and then I was coming.

CHAPTER SEVEN
ADRIK

Every morning I worked out at five am. No exceptions. The routine was so deeply ingrained in my mind, I did not need an alarm. So, when I opened my eyes and peered across the rumpled sheets to find *Zaika moya* gone, I was angry.

Angry but not surprised.

Six days had passed since I had secured Sofia for my one month whatever this was. I did not know what to call it. Privately, it was my wild obsession. It was a behavior so unlike my norm, I did not want to share it with anyone. There did not need to be any witnesses to this madness I felt to possess this woman.

I'd ordered Josef and Marat out of this section of

the triplex penthouse I owned, forbidding entry to any and all without my express and immediate permission. For the first forty-eight hours, we did not leave the bed. I thought for sure I would be tired of her afterwards, that this obsessive hunger I had to possess her would be filled. But that was not the case. Each day I woke up, I wanted her more than ever.

She needed clothes. After I'd ordered my people to her apartment to pack her things—women only were permitted to touch her belongings, otherwise I did not trust the old me to not come out looking for vengeance. God forbid a man touched her panties or even her hairbrush. Beast that I was, I could hardly contain my growl at the thought. I did not share what was mine, and for the next month, Sofia was *mine*.

It was clear the dress she wore, that silver swatch of moonlight that had held me so captivated at the party, had been borrowed. From her former boss, as it turned out. I had it sent back to Missy Castle, dry cleaned and packaged with a thank you note. That woman was bad news, but Zaika did not need to know that.

I had a personal shopper come and measure her, and we discussed some of the places we would be attending over the next month. Sofia was stunned, but silent when the older woman returned from a day of shopping with dozens of things for her. Gowns, suits, pants, sweaters, boots, coats, makeup, heels, you name it.

The one constant was silver. I meant the color. I had asked for silver to be prominent in all the articles of clothing and her accessories. My Zaika looked stunning in silver.

"Are you really telling me what to wear?" she asked, *her brown eyes wide as she glared at me.*

"Yes. I will tell you what goes on that body, and when to take it off," I'd replied.

I proved my point by slamming the laptop closed, cutting off the call with the stylist, and ripping my borrowed t-shirt off her body. Fucking her with my mouth as I pinned her against the wall in the kitchen of my penthouse turned out to be a messy affair.

Breakfast was still on the counter since I'd sent the staff away. I dipped her nipples in fresh whipped cream, licking and sucking until I devoured every drop. By the time I kneeled before her, I was panting. But I was not done. I drizzled honey across her glistening slit, closing my mouth over her clit and sucking until I'd licked her clean.

When she came for me, Sofia screamed my name,

and it was music to my ears. Afterwards, I carried her to the shower and finished the job, fucking her standing up against the glass tile wall.

I'd been staying up to date with business, taking a few phone calls here and there with Andres. After that, I spent all my time with her. At first, I thought she'd been kidding about this *no sleeping with me* rule of hers. Yes, I fucked up. I hated to admit it, but I did. In my proposal, I had assumed sex and sleep were the same. But Sofia, ever the shrewd female, corrected me. Me. Imagine that?

I was the Dark Wolf. I had built my reputation on being ruthless and violent, unhinged in my need for total obedience and my lust for vengeance if crossed. Unhinged, some had said. Even now, in my suit and tie, I made grown men tremble when I entered a boardroom. But she did not fear me. Zaika moya was a brave little bunny, facing off with wolves.

So I made a new deal. If I fucked her hard enough, long enough, wore my Zaika out, then she would remain in my arms all night. Each night, it was a test. Sometimes I did not stop fucking her until the sun came up. My single hope was she would be too exhausted to crawl out of bed to the spare room across the hall, which she'd taken as her own. It was all I could do not to crawl in after her.

But Sofia was an early riser as well. When I went to work out, she was at her laptop, working on her manuscript.

I was dying to get my hands on it, but she told me no, and so far, I respected her wishes. Sofia was a puzzle to me. Full of so many quandaries and complexities, and I was determined to sniff out all her secrets. It was the only way I'd be cured of my unholy obsession with her. At least, that was the hope. So far, each thing I learned only led to more questions that needed answering. Like, how did she know so much about so many things?

She was younger than me, but her mind was amazing. She knew interesting factoids about vastly different subjects, from mythology to architecture and local history. We'd been playing tourist the last few days, and I had to admit it was fun. For over twenty years, I'd lived in this city, but I'd never gone to the Statue of Liberty or the Museum of Natural History, or MOMA. Modern Art was not exactly my forte, but Sofia found excitement everywhere.

We walked for miles, even in the snow, looking at things, talking, exploring. She was a gem. A real wealth of information, my favorite were all the little places she knew that sold delicious little delicacies.

The women who traveled in my circles did not eat in front of men. Most looked like they did not eat at all.

But not Sofia. She was superb in every way. Thick thighs, soft belly, fantastic tits, and an ass that filled my hands. She looked exactly how a woman should. And she felt even better. All that silky softness against my hard body, all that wet warmth surrounding me.

"Fuck," I growled.

My cock sprang to life as my thoughts lingered on her, and I was tempted to jerk off, quiet my raging lust. I adjusted myself, refusing to give in to the temptation to fuck my hand like some teenaged boy. That was another reason I wanted her to sleep with me. I wanted to wake her up with my face buried between her thick thighs, warming her pussy with my tongue and lips. I wanted to tuck her against my body, caging her in as I fucked her from behind before I was even awake.

Yes, I was mad with desire. Unhinged. There was that word again. Maybe it was this game she was playing. Holding out on allowing me to sleep beside her. True, I'd yet to make her stay. I would, though. I was a patient hunter. I got out of bed and stretched, grabbing my workout gear, scrolling through my phone as I went.

"Dammit," I murmured as an urgent message came through.

Andres emailed me with an urgent request from Matthew Castle. It seemed the businessman would not be put off. He wanted to meet with me, and not my brother, and he'd suggested cocktails and dinner tonight at eight. I would have tried to get out of it, but this was important. Frowning, I tugged on my pants and shirt and slid my feet inside my sneakers.

Sofia was on her laptop in the living room, a tray of coffee and biscotti beside her as she typed away. I paused, admiration filling me as I watched her work. She was so beautiful. Her soft features seemed even prettier without paint and glitter. Those precious velvet eyes of hers narrowed as she typed with such dedication.

"Good morning," she said, without looking at me, and I could not help my smile.

She was so polite. So pretty. So soft.

"Morning, Zaika. I'm going to the gym."

"Okay," she replied, distracted.

"We have a dinner party tonight. Cocktails first. Be ready at four."

"Won't you be back before then?" she asked, and this time she looked away from her screen.

I felt ridiculously pleased that she wanted to

spend time with me. At least, that was what I'd hoped. So, I decided another tactic might be in order. Make her wait. Not be so desperate for her. I was the Dark Wolf, not a puppy needing attention from its master.

"No. I will send a car for you. Wear the silk," I ordered, counting on her to know which dress I meant.

Then I left, hoping I was strong enough to stay away from her for the rest of the day.

CHAPTER EIGHT
SOFIA

Adrik had left the penthouse hours ago. It was the perfect opportunity for me to get some basic housekeeping done. I had my book, and it was coming along great. And I needed to call Nonna. But for some reason, all I could do was think about the big bastard.

I had to admit the last few days were not at all horrible. I mean, the man was an exemplary lover. He was attentive, smart, and every time he smiled, which was rare, I felt a ridiculous sense of pride. Like I wanted to crow *look what I did, I made the man smile* to the whole world. I didn't, but I wanted to.

This entire thing was surreal. I was not a femme fatale and men did not move mountains to be with me. But Adrik had certainly manipulated this to his advantage. I couldn't fathom why a man like that was interested. I mean, sure I was pretty. Not spectacular. Not model pretty. But I was attractive, even if I was overweight.

I'd never be skinny. It was just one of those things. I was healthy. I ate fish and vegetables, cooked with olive oil, and tried to walk at least two miles most days. I'd been raised in a good family. Even with the heartache of my mother's death and my father's spiral into alcoholism, Nonna had been there for me. She was a wonderful surrogate for my mom. The building Nonna owned was filled with family, aunts and uncles and cousins, who were my first best friends. My childhood was fairly normal.

When Aunt Linda got married, right as I entered high school, things changed. When Uncle Frank came to live with her, and that bubble of safety I had always felt as a kid just sort of evaporated. I hated calling him that, but the manners taught to me by Nonna were so deeply ingrained it was automatic.

He never did anything. I was not molested in any way. But he was creepy. His eyes would linger on me for too long. Or he'd say something off color to make me squirm. Yeah, I did not like him one bit. Watching him shake when Adrik spoke to him was one of the biggest highlights of my life. I'd waited so long for someone to put the fear of God into that prick.

Who knew my *for the moment* boyfriend was such a badass? I rolled my eyes at the silly title. Adrik was not anyone's boyfriend. Lover. Manipulator. Controller. Those were all better suited to the man. I tried to find out more about him, about his past. But the internet was a fickle bitch, and where on one hand you could find out almost everything about someone with the click of the keys, on the other hand, you had no way of knowing if what you found was true.

Adrik Volkov was rich and powerful. That much I knew. He was intimidating, The way he'd arranged this whole thing was unscrupulous. And yet, there I was. In his penthouse, just like he wanted. I could lie and say I was being held prisoner. But considering I'd gone to bed with him willingly that first night, it would be hypocritical of me to act like I didn't want him.

Honestly, I'd never had someone want me, even if only physically, with the intensity I saw in Adrik's gaze when he looked at me. It was thrilling. Scary, wild, seductive. He made me feel impossibly sexy, wanted. And that was one for the books.

Life was short, and I'd never been lucky in love

or sex. But this was good sex. Fantastic sex. And even if it came with strings, I was human enough to acknowledge how good he made me feel. Jealousy rippled through me at all the women he must have practiced on, but I pushed those thoughts away. Everyone had a past. And I wasn't a virgin, either. It was silly to expect him to be.

I sighed and stood up, stretching. I would not get any more work done, that was certain. I checked the time, and it was already past one. Too early to get ready for four. A walk might do me well. So, I pulled on my boots and new coat, topped it with a hat, scarf, and gloves and headed for the door.

"Sorry, miss, Mr. Volkov did not say you would be going out today."

A guard dressed in all black with several bulges on his person to suggest weapons stopped me at the elevator door, which was located right inside the penthouse. I frowned. Was he serious?

"Well, Mr. Volkov did not say I wouldn't be going out, did he?" I countered.

The man frowned and looked confused. He told me to wait while he spoke into what I assumed was a mic on his cuff. A minute later, a handsome man that I recognized as Adrik's brother came in through the elevator.

"Well, well. Ah, I see. You are the beautiful creature my brother's been keeping locked up. Tired of your cage, princess?" he asked suavely.

I didn't reply right away. No doubt, Marat Volkov was used to sweeping women off their feet, and while I appreciated his purely masculine beauty, he did not move me. So instead of answering, I simply waited for him to continue with whatever game he was playing. All rich men played games. It was a fact, not a theory. And it was one of the foundations for my novel.

"Feisty? I like it. No wonder Adrik is so taken with you. Were you going somewhere?" Marat asked, and I noticed the small twitch in his eye with pleasure.

"Coffee. I was going to the café on the corner," I decided on the spot.

"Would you mind some company, princess? It's been a while since I had the opportunity to visit with such a," he said, looking me up and down in what I assumed was a move most women pined for, "pleasant conversationalist," he finished, tugging on his lower lip with his fingers.

Oh, the guy was good. A practiced flirt, with a handsome hot boy face and rich guy style that garnered him many a heart, I could just tell. He did not strike me as the same sort of man as his brother. There was a teasing air about him, like Marat never took anything seriously. I supposed it was obvious why he didn't. No matter what anyone said, life was a beauty contest, and he was winning.

To me, Adrik was the handsomer of the two. His roughness, that serious, hard edge he had about him made my panties melt right off. But it was his severity that made the joy I felt exuding from him sometimes even more valuable. Marat was still a boy, playing at being a man. But not Adrik. I had the feeling he did not play very much at all. And it made me want to tackle hug him the next time I saw him, wrestle him to the ground and see if I could find a tickle spot.

Christ, I was losing my mind. Imagine me doing that to Adrik!

"As you like," I replied coolly.

Marat's searching stare was making me clench my teeth. He smiled and held out his arm, which I bypassed and walked to the end of the elevator. He spoke to the guard, informed him of where we were going, and stepped a little too close to me inside the elevator. He was tall, thinner than Adrik, and he looked and smelled expensive. Where his brother exuded power and authority, Marat seemed playful and carefree.

I wondered about all the things his brother must have done for him to make his life so smooth. And I wondered if Marat was grateful. Curiosity about the man who'd basically blackmailed me to be his plaything filled me. I wished I could stop it, knowing that way led to trouble and heartache. But I had an active imagination, and it couldn't be helped.

"I never appreciated Adrik's eye for exquisite things before," Marat said, looking me up and down.

"Oh my God, you are not trying to flirt with me, are you?" I said and snorted a laugh.

The poor man looked shocked, but it was just too absurd. A man like Adrik might get caught up in whatever he saw in me, but Marat? No fucking way. He'd have to do better than to pretend to be interested in me to get to whatever it was he was getting at.

"You're a beautiful woman, Sofia. I am sure all men flirt with you," he tried again, regrouping from his first efforts.

"Sure. Men flirt with me. But your brother doesn't strike me as someone who would appreciate this little game you're trying to run, unless he put you up to it," I said.

A dark blush spread across his boyishly handsome face, and I knew he knew he'd been caught. Adrik did not put him up to this. Marat was doing this without big brother's knowledge, or approval, I guessed. He was out for something, and I was curious as to what he thought a nobody like me could possibly know. Maybe it was just an ego thing. I could have saved him the trouble and told him then and there, I was not interested, But I did not think his flirtations were genuine.

"Fine. It is the timing, you understand? We're in the middle of an important deal, Sofia. A deal you are delaying with your presence, and I don't think it is a coincidence you work for Missy Castle," he said, all evidence of the charming young man gone.

"What does my old boss have to do with this?" I asked, my stomach turning.

"Her brother owns the company we are trying to acquire. It is necessary for our interests, but Matthew Castle—"

"Is a total fucking freak," I finished for him.

Oh, I knew all about Matthew Castle, working for Missy. How could I not? She was his younger sister and completely dependent on him. I'd been around more than my fair share of New York's wealthiest and most depraved socialites. That bastard took the cake. He made Uncle Frank look like Santa fucking Clause.

"You know Matthew?" Marat asked, eyes narrowing.

"I met him before. He paid the bills, after all, and I was working as Missy's assistant until she fired me a few days ago."

"After the party?" he asked.

"Yes, after the party. I figured Adrik arranged it so I would accept his deal. But I have no idea what business you or Adrik have with him, Marat. I mean it."

"And I suppose I should just take your word for it," he scoffed.

We walked side by side down the busy Manhattan street to the small Italian café where I'd gotten a delicious macchiato the day before with Adrik. I missed him, I realized which was stunning and disheartening, as I waited for my coffee.

"Okay, a few things," I began as I slid into the chair Marat held out for me. "I have no idea about any deals. Adrik doesn't talk to me about business."

"Then what are you doing here? Is it about the clothes? The dates? Money? I have money, Sofia, and I can pay you—"

"Stop it," I growled, insulted. "I am really tired of

you people trying to buy me. Adrik and I have an arrangement. He's helping my family out over a rough patch in return for my agreeing to spend the next month with him. Three weeks now," I said, and tried to ignore the pang in my heart at the mention of time.

"One month? Wait. The properties he bought, that was for you?" he asked, eyebrows raised.

Though he was speaking in a low, hushed tone, I could not help but feel like I was on display. Women around us, even some of the men, did not hide the fact they were checking Marat out. I supposed they could not be blamed. He was very pretty. But right then, I hated him. Hated what he was forcing me to come face to face with, and that was my own delusions.

"I didn't ask him to buy anything. He'd already made the purchases when he propositioned me."

"Propositioned? So, he did pay for your time? You know, it is a puzzle, Sofia. My brother is one of the most sought after men in the world. He is rich and powerful. He can have anyone he wants by snapping his fingers. You know, I looked you up. And I cannot figure it out. Why does he want you so? You have fucked him already. This, I know. He spent two days locked in that penthouse, ignoring business, just to have sex with you," he said, eyeing me like I was a maggot.

"The only thing I can think of that is holding his interest is your connection to Castle, unless," he said.

He was letting the last word hang there as he looked at me again, like he was trying to imagine my naked body and what attractions I could possibly hold for any man, let alone his esteemed brother.

Conceited much?

"Missy fired me before my arrangement with Adrik started. As for what interests him, you should ask your brother," I said.

Hurt and anger had my eyes filling with unshed tears. I was stunned. Hurt even by the likelihood that Marat's assessment of my deal with Adrik seemed valid.

"Forgive me for being crude, but he is my brother. Adrik is everything to me. How do I know someone else can't buy you?" he asked, and anger flashed in his eyes.

"Fuck you for thinking I am some whore anyone can buy," I hissed.

He wasn't exactly wrong about Adrik and me. Maybe that was why I felt so ugly inside. So angry. Here I was, living in some little vacuum, pretending I was the star in my very own dark romance and that my relationship with Adrik might turn into something else. Something that started with sex but maybe ended with something more.

I was a fucking idiot. Marat was right. Adrik had bought me, and for the first time in my life, I felt like a whore.

"You seem angry. Sofia. Did I insult you? I must apologize, you see, my brother does not have weaknesses. He does not show emotions. But this last week, he has not been himself," he said as if that's any explanation.

"Excuse me. I think I need to get back," I murmured, neglecting to pick up my coffee.

"Miss? Miss, you have to pay for this!" the barista called, but I was too upset to stop.

"Sofia! Wait! Fuck," I heard Marat growl, but I looked back and saw him paying for the coffee.

Good. I would hate to think the café got stiffed. But I was just too emotional to speak. Shame washed over me. I'd been caught up, romanticizing what Adrik and I were doing in my head. Physically, I liked it very much. But I was getting attached, building castles in the sky, starting to believe this was something it wasn't.

Shit. This was dangerous territory. I was being foolish. I'd made a deal, and I couldn't leave no matter how much I wanted to. It was time for me to stop pretending Adrik and I were dating.

We weren't. This wasn't that kind of story. He'd paid me to keep his bed warm, and that was what I would do. I would fuck him when he said, go with him to dinner parties or whatever, and the rest of the time I would stay in the spare bedroom.

No more traipsing around Manhattan and getting dim sum in Chinatown. No more museums and outings. No more trying to earn his smiles. No more ammunition for breaking my heart.

I couldn't risk it. His was not my world. I didn't know how to play these kinds of games. How would I go back to my ordinary life afterwards if I fell for the man? There was no possibility he would fall for me. I was not in his league. Not even remotely. But why would it matter? I did not love him, I told myself, angry at myself for even thinking it.

My phone buzzed, and I looked down. Nonna had returned my text. She was happy, safe, and I was glad. I should have called her, but I couldn't talk just yet. The elevator ride was quick, and I ignored the guards and went to the bedroom where I had them put my new clothes.

It was showtime. I was just playing dressing up. Acting a part. Yeah, I could do that. Just like drama class in high school. Fuck Marat for trying to play me into revealing some stupid corporate espionage plot. I was no spy. I was just a chubby Jersey girl who'd caught the eye of his billionaire brother.

Something he wanted to have, to borrow really, just for a little while. Like a piece of art or some other oddity. I was a temporary possession, rented, used, and when it was over, I would be sent back. Those thoughts played over and over in my head the entire time I showered and dressed, readying myself for this dinner party, whatever it was.

I took care to do my hair and makeup, using an iron to make fat, glossy, sable-colored curls cascading over my shoulders. I wore the silver silk dress he'd told me to wear.

It was simple in design, resembling a long slip with spaghetti straps that crisscrossed over my back. My shoulders were small, and they'd been taken in for me that day. All of my clothes had been fitted and adjusted to fit my shorter, wider frame. The dress felt delicious against my skin. So soft, so fine, and so thin you could see my nipples despite the teddy I wore beneath it.

It fell to my ankles in a flutter of silver fabric that moved when I walked and made me feel like I was floating on a cloud. But that was just more fiction. I was very much on solid ground. I slipped on the strappy matching heels with the infamous red sole and wondered at how comfortable they were despite being ridiculously high.

Those shoes cost more than my rent, and though I'd seen them in stores in the city, I'd never thought I would own a pair. Much less the twelve pairs Adrik had ordered for me. I hoped he would get more use out of them, since there was no way I would take any of the clothes or shoes with me after the month was up. Maybe his next plaything would be my size. The thought made my heart squeeze painfully in my chest.

Last, I gathered the 1920s style velvet robe that went on top of the dress and waited for Adrik to arrive. It was five minutes to four when I walked into the living room, and he was already there wearing a black tuxedo. Our eyes met and suddenly the room felt very small. He lowered his gaze, dragging it from my head to my feet, and I swore I felt the air sizzle with desire.

I might not have understood the game, but after my meeting with Marat, I was better prepared to steel myself against the unwanted tug on my heartstrings from such a look. If only this was a different sort of meeting. If only he hadn't manipulated things so I had no choice but to be with him for this short time. Regret scratched at me, but I forced it away.

But all the *if onlys* would not get me through the next month. It was better to put on a smile and pretend I was as unaffected by him as he was by me. Adrik Volkov was a wolf who did not bother with sheep's clothing. He wanted my body, and I agreed to give it to him. For one month.

I just had to remember to stick to that.

CHAPTER NINE
ADRIK

It almost killed me staying away all day. The temptation to barge in on her and rip her from whatever she was doing just so I could feel her mouth on mine, her skin against my sin, hear her whimpers and swallow her cries was so damn strong, I spent an extra hour working out just to control the impulse.

Then, it was a matter of not texting or calling her. A true test of my control, you might say. That I wound up breaking my phone to refrain from using it, I would not mention to anyone else. Andres had no problem replacing it within the hour, which was how I'd spent the remainder of the afternoon. Waiting on the Apple Store to deliver their latest and greatest.

Not that I had to wait. But I did have to stay away from Sofia. For my own sanity's sake. Fuck, how I thought of that woman. All day long. What was she doing? Did she miss me like I missed her?

The pair of panties I'd plucked from her body the night before were still in my pocket. I'd touched them through the day, squeezing the lacy softness and lifting them to my face so I could smell her sweet pussy while I pretended to concentrate on work.

Volkov Industries was a well-oiled machine that required little interference. But I was the president. The head. And nothing happened without my knowledge or approval. So yes, I was distracted, but I got the job done. Marat came in sometime after lunch and bombarded me with a barrage of questions about Sofia. But she was not his business. She was mine. Mine alone.

I arrived back, dressed in my tux having changed in the office, at ten to four. I wanted to knock down the door to the bedroom she'd claimed as her own, but I forced myself to have a drink instead. Good thing, too. Because when Sofia finally walked out of the bedroom dressed in silk as silver as moonlight, it was all I could do not to drop to my knees, toss my head back and howl for her like the goddess she was.

The velvet coat she dragged behind her looked soft as her skin, warm, too, which was good. It was freezing outside. I would not want her cold. Remembering the state of her frigid apartment caused anger to rise in my veins, but I pressed it down. My people had already dealt with most of the issues on that property and her grandmother's. When she went back—fuck. I did not like to think about that. When her time with me was over.

"Are you ready?" she asked, her soft voice sifting through the air, breaking my train of thought.

"Da, Zaika."

I held out my arm, and she stepped forward, pausing to shrug on the velvet coat. My cock hardened as I stared, watching the way the silk clung to her shapely form. I frowned hard. I should not have asked her to wear that dress outside of my penthouse. She looked far too good in it.

The silk clung to her curves like a second skin. Her nipples pressed against the fabric, and I wondered if it felt good to her. I wanted to test it out for myself. To rub the expensive fabric over her mounds and her cleft, to see if she was as wet for me now as I was hard for her. But I needed to wait to sate my hunger till after this pretentious dinner party. I could not touch her then bring her there.

Could not risk having others witness the serene look on her face that always came after she did. Her post orgasm expressions were mine. I did not share. Not ever.

So, I steeled my face, refusing to show expression as we rode the elevator to the limo waiting below. The ride to the Castle estate would be long. But worth it. The quicker we got this over with, the quicker I would have her back in my arms. In my bed. And perhaps tonight she would stay the whole night. The possibility made me eager. I looked forward to the challenge of it.

I did not notice at first, so caught up in my own desires, that my Zaika was unusually quiet. I attempted small talk, trying to draw her out. But other than one worded answer and polite smiles, she did not engage. It was unusual, and my frown deepened. It took over an hour to drive out to Long Island, and the entire time, she avoided eye contact with me.

Did something happen that I was not privy to? Something to make her go quiet? I frowned hard. If there was a problem, I wanted to know, needed to fix it. It was not a look I liked on my otherwise bubbly Sofia. It bothered me she did not come to me with her problem. If there was one. My brain was now fixated on this.

Sofia usually talked my head off with little bite-sized facts about this or that. She was full of questions. Like a walking, talking inquisition. She was relentless, prying information from me like pearls from oysters. I did not share world secrets, but I did not mind talking about things I did. I was not ashamed of who I was. And she should know exactly who was fucking her each night. Her brain was active, her imagination, too. And I loved learning about what made her tick. Fuck. I should not be using that word. This was temporary. Still, I could not help it. My obsession was growing, not getting better.

I took my new phone from my breast pocket and sent a text to Josef. He was the head of security, and though I ordered the cameras in the guest bedroom to be turned off for the duration of her stay, the rest of the house, save my bedroom, was completely wired. Something must have happened to my Zaika to make her this quiet shell of herself.

My phone buzzed as the driver pulled up to the Castle estate where instead of a private dinner party the man was hosting a goddamned party. I waited till we were standing in the receiving line indoors to look at what Josef sent me. Pictures of my brother's smiling face and my Zaika laughing at something he said filled my screen, and I felt rage building inside my blood.

Fury. Jealousy. And some other choice emotions rolled through me as we moved up in line to where a woman in black stood to take our coats.

"Adrik?" Sofia said my name, and I looked up.

My fury must have been clear on my face if her reaction was anything to go by. She moved back a step, like the frightened bunny I once thought she was. Her velvet eyes darted left and right, but who could save her from me? It would have been laughable if I wasn't shaking with my rage.

Had my brother seduced my Zaika while I worked myself into a lathering sweat just to stay away? I needed to know. But now was not the time or place. It had happened rarely where Marat had been interested in one of my castoffs. But he always asked permission first. Always made sure I was okay with it. This I was not okay with. This I might hurt him for. Or worse.

Killing my brother was off the table. But with a face like that, perhaps he could afford to lose a limb. A finger? A hand? It would depend on what he did. The thought of his hands on her soft, pale skin had me picturing the horrible things I would do to him, or to anyone who dared touch her while she was mine.

Hell. If I was going to keep this madness to myself, then I could admit in my own head that I was almost certain my obsession with Zaika would not be quenched soon. If ever.

Unhinged.

The word flashed in my brain like a neon sign. Or one of those digital billboards in Times Square. Yes. Perhaps I was unhinged.

If I was contemplating maiming my brother while accepting a glass of whiskey from a passing server, then yes, I would say unhinged was an apt description. Sofia took a glass of champagne, smiling tightly as she looked around the room. It was full of men and women who were part of the establishment. I recognized many of the faces but did not bother saying hello or making introductions when they were bold enough to approach us.

My fingers itched to touch her. To feel her body trembling beneath the moonlight silk she wore, but I did not trust myself to stop there. I burned for her. Wanted to impale her on my cock and remove the stain of my brother's hands on her skin.

Perhaps if I touched another, if I held another

woman, fucked someone else, maybe then I would not feel that insane jealousy. I could do that there. I could crook my finger and have any woman in the vicinity willing to drop her panties for me in front of the whole fucking crowd. Did Sofia not understand that?

Maybe, I thought as I walked towards the dance floor. Just maybe it was time to teach her who I was. Wolf not man. Bastard, not just billionaire.

I heard Sofia walking beside me, her heels clicking on the marble tiles, creating a seductive tattoo that pounded inside my brain. There was a live band playing, and people writhing on the floor. Society's elite, I scoffed.

"Wait here," I ordered, not bothering to look at Sofia while I grabbed the hand of a scantily clad woman.

Yes, some of the women were hired to be there. Professionals. Escorts. And this one, I recognized. Her flashy red nails looked gauche against my black jacket, and her perfume was cloying, burning my nostrils. But I pulled her into my body, holding her tight as I danced her across the floor. I needed to prove to Sofia I did not depend on her. She needed to be reminded of her place. Or maybe it was me who needed to be reminded.

I looked up, not surprised to see she'd left. I stepped away from the woman I'd been dancing with and hunted my Zaika across the floor. A flash of silver caught my eye, and I watched her scurry into the ladies' room, a snarl on my lips as I followed.

"Adrik! Glad you could make it, old boy."

Matthew Castle stopped my progress with his hand outstretched. I glared at it before I remembered where I was and what I was there for. Clearing my throat, I took his hand and gave it a hard shake that left the weaker man noticeably paler.

"Castle," I replied, nodding at the woman beside him.

It was his sister. Missy Castle. Her eyes roamed over me like I was a piece of meat, and I wanted to snap at her to keep her eyes in her head, but I refrained. Upsetting my host was not a good idea, especially when it was his company I needed.

"I thought this was a dinner party," I said.

"Yes, well, it was supposed to be, but my dear sister thought this might be better. After all, you Russians like a good party, no?"

"I am American, now, Matthew. Even when I was living in Russia, I was only half," I said, giving away just enough to shock the man into silence.

I knew he'd been digging into my past, looking

for a way to blackmail me into sweetening the deal. Truth was, regardless of how old and prominent their family name, Matthew Castle was grossly in debt. CoreTech was the last thing he had of value. I was not trying to swindle him, but I would not be blackmailed by anyone.

Foolish man did not know what I really was before the designer suits, limousines, and penthouses. The word mafia had been tossed around, but that word did not apply. I was not part of a gang or a crime family. Never had been What I had gained in life, position, money, power, was all of my own making. Any criminal activity I had been involved in was for me and Marat, my brother, who I really needed to talk to.

Mobsters owed fealty to someone, something higher than themselves. In my world, there was no one higher. I was no mobster. I was worse than that.

CHAPTER TEN
SOFIA

"Fucking motherfucker," I whispered and sniffed.

"Miss?" a woman dressed in all black handed me a tissue.

"Thanks," I replied, dabbing the skin beneath my eyes so I wouldn't smear my makeup.

It was stupid. I was stupid. Crying over a man who had literally bought me because he was dancing with some skinny ho. Shit. That wasn't nice. I never wanted to be the kind of woman who called other women hos just cause they were flashy and liked a different aesthetic than me. I didn't know the woman. I just hated her the second she touched him. Fuck. That didn't make me any better, did it?

"Are you okay, miss?" the restroom attendant asked.

"Yes. I'm sorry. Thank you," I said, and she nodded towards the door.

I heard the clicking of heels and knew I was about to have company. With some of the people I'd observed at this party, it was likely someone I did not know. Still, it wouldn't do to be seen crying in here. Like a sap. So, I washed my hands and patted my face, made sure I was presentable.

"Oh, my God! Did you see who I was dancing with? That was Adrik Volkov, the billionaire," the woman in red whisper-screamed to her friend.

I tried to ignore their chatter about who was there and what they were worth, but it made my skin crawl. It was like all they could see hanging over the head of every man they talked about were dollar signs. I shivered. Was that what it was like to be Adrik? How awful.

And how was I any better? I'd allowed him to buy me things. To rescue my family from debt. I'd sold him my company. Accepted money in exchange for my time. Shit. I was the ho, and the realization made me nauseous. Suddenly, the smells of perfume and cologne, the drink I had after we walked in, and the lack of dinner caught up with me. I felt dizzy, and sick to my stomach. I needed to get out of there.

Exiting the ladies' room, I scanned the floor and did not see Adrik. We were all the way out in Long Island, and I did not know how I would get back to the city. But I could not stay there. My heels clacked on the stone steps outside the mansion, and I gasped at how cold it was. Fuck. I left my coat behind. But that was too bad for me. Maybe the cold air would offer some clarity. I took off faster than I would've thought possible on heels, removing them once my feet touched the icy sand behind the sprawling estate as I raced towards the water.

I dropped the expensive shoes as I ran closer to where the freezing waves crashed onto the shore. It was easy to forget we were so close to nature, so close to something as wild as the sea when in the big city. This mansion was in a prime spot, located right on the Long Island Sound. But I did not care about the opulent estate.

Adrik had danced with another woman. His big, calloused hands had touched her. His lips quirked up in a sexy smirk when she'd whispered to him. She'd been beautiful, so thin and tall. She looked perfect beside him.

Oh fuck. My heart was breaking. How could I be

so stupid as to form an attachment to him? I felt like my soul was being devoured by feelings I couldn't control. Feelings as wild as the icy cold water that was wetting the bottom of my dress and freezing my toes. The moon hung low in the sky, the silvery light bathing the water with stunning, ethereal beauty. I was trying to find my breath, but it was so cold I might as well have been trying to breathe in ice.

"Zaika!"

I gasped and spun around just as his big hands closed over my arms. He cursed roughly, picking me up and crushing me to him as he kicked through the backwash of the retreating waves. His shoes would be ruined, I thought inanely as heat from his body seeped into mine.

"Adrik, I—"

"Not one word, Zaika," he growled, and carried me across the sand to a paved road where the limo was waiting for us.

Josef was there, his face grim. He opened the door, closing it after Adrik placed me on the seat, and climbed in after me. He did not allow me to sit alone, grabbing me and pulling me back on his lap. I was shaking and wet, and miserable. But when I tried to speak, to explain, he cut me off once more.

"Nyet."

His strong arms wrapped around me, and I noticed he'd removed his jacket at some point, before or after he came after me, I did not know. He grabbed the velvet coat off the seat in front of us, wrapping it around my frozen body and rubbing his hands up and down my arms. I had no idea who'd retrieved it for me, but I was glad. Just as I was glad to see my shoes sitting on the floor.

The heat was on full blast, but I couldn't feel it yet. The mesmerizing sound of Adrik breathing heavily as he tried to rub the feeling back into my limbs was making me swoon. I couldn't help it. I was so turned on, when his hands cupped my face and he brought my cheek to press against his, I turned to catch his lips.

Once I started kissing him, that was it. I could not stop. He groaned as I turned in his lap, pressing against the hard bar beneath his pants. My dress was wet along the bottom, and I'd bunched it up around my waist so I could straddle him. It was cold and uncomfortable around my back and belly, but it was worth it just to feel his hard body pressed so closely to mine.

"Sofia," he whispered my name, my real name, and not the pet one he used for me, and I trembled with need.

Desire roared through me like a blazing inferno, My pussy clenched, dripping moisture, ruining his expensive pants, but I didn't care. I needed him.

"Adrik. Adrik, please," I begged, going out of my mind.

"You need me, Zaika. Tell me where," he commanded. Lifting my dress and pulling it over my head.

"Here," I said, pressing his face to my silk covered breasts.

"You're wrapped up like a present, Zaika, just for me," he growled with a fierceness that should have terrified me, but it only made me want him more.

Adrik's chest rumbled as he caught my silk-clad nipple and sucked it into his mouth. I groaned, unable to be silent. His fingers dug into my ass, and I pressed down, needing to feel him. Bastard held me still, didn't allow me to swerve or grind as I wanted to. He bit my breast, and I cried out, the brief pain only bringing me that much higher.

"Where else do you need me, Zaika? Here?" he asked, sliding his hand between us, teasing my pussy with his fingers.

I nodded, desperate for him.

"Did you fuck my brother?" he asked, and I stopped moving.

I was seconds from coming with only the lightest of pressure from his fingertips, and I could not believe my ears. The fact I froze must have solidified whatever misconception he had, because he ripped the bottom of the teddy, plunging two fingers into me without pause.

"Did you get hot and wet for him too, Zaika?" he growled, his fury clear even as he fucked me with his hand.

I wanted to scream. To hit him. To make him stop. But he held me firmly in his steel embrace, keeping me against him. My traitorous body trembled, wanting more from him, and I thought I was going to be sick.

"Did you come for him? Did Marat watch your eyes turn molten when you have your pleasure? Tell me!" he snarled, but he never stopped working his fingers in and out, a mockery of what we shared.

"No! I didn't fuck, Marat."

"Tell the truth," he snarled, grabbing my face with the fingers he just pulled from my pussy. I smelled myself on him, felt the sticky wetness of my arousal as it clung to my cheeks.

"It is the truth. Marat walked me to the café and tried to flirt with me to get information. He thinks I'm a corporate spy. But I told him the truth. I'm just someone you wanted to fuck. Just a stupid, easy woman you bought so you don't have to work at pretending to be in a relationship," I snapped, feeling shattered.

"Stop. Stop, Zaika," he whispered, and I realized I was squirming trying to get off his lap.

"You stop. You stop, Adrik. Let me go," I said, needing to get away from him to force my body to stop feeling.

The sick feeling in the pit of my stomach that he could believe I'd fucked his brother was not going away. I would not forget it. But my body was a slave to his. I couldn't stop my ready submission or reactions from happening, and I tried. Believe me, I tried.

"No, I will not. You are mine. Mine," he growled. "I'm going to remind you who you belong to."

My eyes widened as he pushed me onto the seat opposite us. My bare ass hit the cold leather, and I hissed, but that was all I had time for because Adrik was on his knees, his face buried in my pussy. He went at me like a beast, and I reveled in his uncontrolled urgency.

Never in my life did I ever expect to elicit such a response from a man, any man, never mind him. Adrik Volkov. The Dark Wolf. He growled while sucking and licking at my sex, sending vibrations rocketing through my body starting with my clit. My orgasm slammed into me, hard and fast, and I yelled his name while clawing at his shoulders. But he didn't stop then, he continued to lap at my slit, sucking down all my juices until he lifted his head, his chin glossy with it. I panted, watching him as he dipped down again, his tongue snaking out of his mouth.

"It's too much," I moaned, trying to wiggle away, but his big hand gripped me tight. Too tight for me to do anything but stay right where he wanted me. And if I were honest, it was what I wanted too.

"You can take it, Zaika. You will take it. As many as I give to you, you will take them. That's it. Your pussy is rippling already. Good girl. Now, come for me again," he said, and my legs started to shake on either side of his head.

I did not think I had it in me. But as his fingers filled my heated core, moving in time with his long licks, I discovered I was wrong. Apparently, I could come again. And I did. Several times.

CHAPTER ELEVEN
ADRIK

After all the shit that went on, the raging emotions I'd been feeling all night, I finally wore Zaika moya out. I slid her still damp dress over her head and lifted her in my arms, draping the velvet coat around her. Boarding the private elevator to my penthouse, I had Josef hand me her shoes and had him carry my jacket. I could not bring myself to allow another man to hold any part of her. Not even her clothing.

"Do you still want me to bring Marat?" he asked in a hushed whisper.

I nodded, kissing Sofia's forehead when she whimpered and snuggled closer. She said no to fucking my brother. But I still needed to confront him. He'd left my penthouse with her. Talked to her about me, about us and whatever he'd said, it had changed something.

Jealousy was not a familiar emotion. I did not feel it often. And yet, because of her, I found myself falling into fits of envy that were nothing like me. I was still vibrating with energy, even after making her come three times on my mouth and once on my fingers alone during the drive. My dick was rock hard, but I refused to sate myself until I spoke with my brother.

The elevator slid open silently, just another perk for the wealthy. And I strode across the penthouse, depositing my Zaika on top of the mattress. I removed the damp dress and ruined teddy carefully, so as not to jostle her from her slumber. I forced myself to look away, knowing if I stared at her creamy pale softness, I would not be able to help myself.

Fuck. She was sublime. A beautiful goddess made from moonlight. I was in her thrall. Knowing it and living it did not make it any easier. But I would do terrible things for this woman. And I was about to.

I closed the bedroom door and sauntered to the living room where Marat was casually slung across the sofa. He was rumpled, wearing silk pajama bottoms and nothing else, possibly drunk, but I did not care.

"What is it, brother? I thought you were at Castle's dinner tonight."

"What did you do today, Marat?" I asked, staring down at him expressionless.

"Do? What do you mean? I did what I always do. Work, dinner, party, went home with a woman, who is now sleeping in my bed cause this fuck woke me up and said you wanted to talk to me. So, what do you want?" Marat scoffed.

"That's all. You didn't come here? Maybe go for a walk? For coffee? With Sofia," I growled her name.

Marat blanched as he stared at me, realization dawning. I took a step towards him, and my brother raised his hands, shaking his head. But it was too late. Even if he didn't fuck her, he needed to know, to understand there were some real consequences for flirting.

"You're my brother," I growled.

"Adrik! I swear, I did nothing. It's not what you think!" he gasped as I grabbed the back of his neck and hauled him to his feet. "I didn't touch her! I thought she was a s-spy. I wanted to protect you!"

"You don't want to do this, Adrik. I know what

Marat means to you. Let him go," a soft voice said from behind me.

I turn my head away from the sight of my hand choking my brother to Zaika moya. She was wearing one of my workout shirts. It was long enough to cover her nudity, probably the only thing she could find since she refused to keep her clothes in my bedroom. It was an undershirt, thin, white. And if the lights were on, I had no doubt I'd be able to see right through it. In fact, if I looked hard enough, I could. Which meant they could.

I dropped Marat on the floor and stalked over to her, moving her behind me. She didn't protest, simply wrapped her arms around my waist and pressed her front to my back as if she too realized her attire left her open to other eyes when my gaze had dropped to her breasts.

"Fuck! Dammit, Adrik! I would never disrespect you like that," Marat said hoarsely, sitting up and rubbing his neck.

Josef was leaning against the wall, watching the byplay with seemingly little interest. I frowned at him, and he shrugged.

"You wouldn't have killed him. But just in case," he said and waved the gun he'd been holding in his left hand. "Rubber rounds," he explained, looking past me.

I realized he was talking to Sofia when she squeezed me tighter and her horrified gasp sounded next to my ears. Was she worried about my wellbeing? That was new. Usually, I was the one taking care of everyone around me. It was an odd thing having someone care whether I lived or died.

"I told you, nothing happened with Marat," Sofia said, and I rumbled my reply.

"No, he is right, Sofia. If someone took my woman out without my permission, I would be upset, too. I will tell you the truth, brother, this little bunny as you call her, is more like a she-wolf. Ferocious, brother. She gave as good as she got and she never said a word against you," Marat said, dragging himself off the floor.

Still, I did not reply. I couldn't. My feelings were still very volatile, and I didn't trust myself to act rationally yet. Marat avoided looking at Sofia when he walked towards me, then he held out his hand.

"Congrats, brother," he said, and I shook his proffered hand, not sure what I was accepting his congratulations for.

He nodded at me, clicking his tongue behind his teeth. Then Josef and Marat left, and I was alone with her. Her arms were still wrapped around me in a sort of hug, and the feel of her soft tits pressed against my back made me aware of the fact I still had not come. After bringing her to several orgasms, it was crazy to think I still hungered for more.

But that was the nature of obsession, wasn't it? It made little sense, defied all logic, and it endured. Like the motherfucking Twinkie of emotions. That shit could outlast nuclear war.

The lights of Manhattan glittered below us, but I was not looking at the view. I was looking at her. The expression on her face as she hugged my body to hers. Three weeks. That was all the time I had left with her, and I was done with pretenses. No more interruptions. No more pretending to be at work when my mind was only on her.

"Adrik, I'm sorry," she began.

I turned to face her, regretting the loss of her touch immediately. My face marred in a frown as I'm trying to understand what the hell she was apologizing for. Was it for making me lose my fucking mind? Cause that was on me. Not her. I was not a good person. I was not born to be good. I was ruthless. Hard. Hunter. Wolf.

Sofia was good. She deserved good. She deserved everything. Not a man who used bribery and manipulations to get her into spending a month with him. But I couldn't make myself take it back. Especially not looking at her wearing my undershirt over her naked body.

"Why sorry, Zaika?" I asked.

"I don't want you to be upset with Marat. He's your brother and your relationship is worth a lot more than a month with me," she said, and that confession damn near broke me.

"Are you sorry about this?" I asked, needing to know.

"I just apologized—oh, you mean about this, not about your brother," she answered her own question. "I suppose I could lie to you and say I hate you, hate this, but the truth is, I've never been the object of someone's desire."

"I do not think that can be true, Zaika."

"Well, think what you like, but no one has ever pursued me quite like you. And just cause we're being honest," she said, stepping closer, tracing her hand down my chest, abs, and settling her hot little palm over the bulge in my pants. "I really like your dick, Adrik. A lot."

I was frozen in the middle of the living room, her hand on my cock. I was hard already, but having her whisper such things made me even harder. A sultry grin tipped the corners of her lips upward, and she held my gaze as she undid my pants, pushing them down with a swoosh.

"Sofia," I growled her name, but did not stop her when she dropped to her knees.

"Adrik," she whispered, her hands unleashing my cock from its confines.

Her eyes widened and darkened with desire while she stroked and gripped me at the base. She leaned forward, plump lips parted and sucked my head right into her hot, wet mouth, pulling precum straight from my balls. I groaned aloud. So fucking turned on, it was all I could do not to grab her head and ram my cock all the way down her throat.

This was the first time she'd started things between us. The first time she'd initiated sex. I let her go at her own pace, allowed her to explore me for as long as I could. Her mouth was so hot, her groans so damn seductive as she took me inside her mouth, sucking on my head and releasing it with a popping sound.

Then, as if she couldn't take the teasing anymore, she did what I'd been desperate for her to do. Zaika moya held my stare as she cupped my balls with one hand, took my cock in the other, and deep throated me as far as she could without gagging.

"That's it, Zaika, take my dick, take it all," I growled, taking over.

Cupping my hand behind her head, I held her still and fucked her mouth. I'd had blowjobs before, some from women whose only job was to give them. Talented women. Gifted even. But nothing could compare to the whimpers and moans I conjured from that sexy sweet mouth as Sofia sucked my dick while on her knees with a perfect view of Manhattan behind her. My moonlight goddess. Zaika moya.

"Tell me now, want me to come in your mouth or no," I groaned, almost losing it completely.

I released her head, giving her the choice, but she did not stop. Her head kept bobbing as she sucked, and she squeezed my shaft and balls with her hands, and then it was too late to move. I was coming and coming, warm ropes of cum flooding her mouth.

I came harder than I ever did before, and my sweet Zaika slurped it all down. Swallowing my essence like it was the most delicious thing she ever tasted. I sank to my knees in front of her, exhausted and elated. And I claimed her lips, tasting my salty essence as I kissed her deeply showing her without words how much what she'd just done meant to me.

I carried her to the bedroom, never breaking our kiss except to remove certain articles of clothing out of the way. And when we were naked, rolling together like waves in the ocean, I continued to kiss her. I couldn't get enough. My earlier jealousy had been misplaced, but at least I was able to admit it. And if I could do that, I could admit there was something deeper going on here. Something more than just sex.

"Stay."

The words left me before I could tell my stupid brain to shut the fuck up. I'd spent the last hour with my cock balls deep inside my beautiful Zaika. Her luscious thighs were still wrapped around my body, and her pussy rippled with every subtle move I made, as if she couldn't stop coming for me.

"Sleep here, with me, Zaika moya."

"No," she replied, and hurt filled my chest.

"You want to. I know you do."

"I do want to, Adrik," she confessed, and elation filled me.

"Then do it. Stay till morning with me. Sleep all night long in my arms," I growled, nuzzling her lips with mine.

"You know I won't."

Her velvet brown eyes searched mine and my heart thudded heavily inside my chest. Why did she keep doing this to us? Why did she keep pushing me away?

"Sleep by my side," I implored her one last time.

"I can't, Adrik," she said, and fuck me, I did not understand her at all.

"Why?" I asked, the words leaving my lips without permission again.

I was fucking begging her. Did she not understand what that meant? Men in my position with my lifestyle did not beg. Not ever. She shook her head and her velvet brown eyes filled with tears. Fuck. She was breaking my heart with that expression. As if I were the one telling her no.

"It is easy, no? To stay. There is a pillow for you, a blanket, sheets. Are they not to your liking? Want me to order a different thread count? Color? What is it?"

"I can't stay," she said again, sobs catching in her throat. "If I sleep beside you tonight, tomorrow. It won't be enough, Adrik. I'll be addicted. If I sleep beside you, I won't want to sleep alone ever again," she said and pushed against my chest.

I was stunned, so I allowed it. Rolling to the side, and watching her as she left my bed, my room, and me alone in the dark to ponder. I could not move. Her confession had gutted me. Could it be all this while I'd been so focused on this all-consuming passion I had for her I missed something? That I had missed the part where she was a person with feelings and emotions beyond her control.

I had to do better for the both of us. I vowed to do better. But the deal was precarious and the mines we held claim to overseas were under fire. Business was taking up more time than I had allotted for, but there was nothing else to be done.

The next week flew by in a haze of work, take-out, and sex. As if we'd made some verbal deal, which we hadn't. Zaika moya seemed to know what I needed each day when I came back from my grueling conference calls and meetings with heads of state and bastard CEOs. Matthew Castle was being a right prick, and I wished I was the Dark Wolf again. I would end that motherfucker faster than he could blink.

But I forgot all about him and CoreTech and the rest the second I was back inside my penthouse with her. She'd started doing this thing where she'd be plating our dinner in nothing but an apron, and I'd wind up eating her first. I'd started stripping in the elevator to save time because I was so desperate to be inside her.

I hadn't seen her with clothes on for the last forty-eight hours and after we fucked, we'd eat and play a guessing game. I'd try to guess what she had on that day, and if I won, I'd get to take her panties with me to work the next morning. I fucking loved that game.

She did not leave the penthouse without me. Not for anything. But it did not seem to bother her. I kept her up most nights, hating the fact I would eventually nod off and she would leave me, but operating on less than two hours of sleep was taking its toll. I'd taken to napping in my office after my workout because if I was home, I would want to be with her, in her. I could not help myself. I was wild for her, and insatiable. Our time was speeding by. I could practically see it like sand falling through an hourglass.

It was like a honeymoon without the wedding. I loved being inside of her, but it drove me crazy she would not stay in my arms throughout the night. She fell asleep beside me a few times, but always snuck out after I fell asleep. I might have started this thing, thinking I could fuck her out of my system. Only, I was starting to suspect I had fucked her even deeper into it.

Sofia was on my mind all the time. But it wasn't an unwelcome invasion of my space and energy. No, I looked forward to it, to her. To seeing her, tasting her, fucking her, hell, just being with her. My obsession was growing, and there was nothing I could do about it. I did not think I even wanted to try to stop it anymore. Zaika moya was becoming necessary to my existence.

But I only had two weeks left of our arrangement. Two weeks, then she would be gone. If I allowed it. The prospect filled me with determination, but business would not be put off any longer.

I had to work in order to play. That was the story of my life. Zaika moya was mine for now, and it would have to suffice. Once I closed the deal on CoreTech, I could focus all my energy on her. Then there would be no going back. I was going to keep my moonlight goddess. Tie her to the fucking bed if it was the only way to make her stay. She had no idea those thoughts were going on in my head, if she did, she might have run from me. Even so, it was too late.

My obsession was mine, and I intended to keep her.

CHAPTER TWELVE
SOFIA

I fidgeted with the hem of my dress. It was clingy and short, but it made my boobs look good with its plunging neckline and long-sleeves. The heels on my feet accentuated my legs, making them look longer, and I crossed them, grinning when Adrik's gaze zeroed right on my ass.

"Do not sit like that when we are out," he growled, and I lifted an eyebrow. "Please, unless you want me to kill someone tonight you will not cross your legs like that at dinner."

"Okay," I agreed. "But you bought me this dress, and you picked it out for me to wear tonight."

"I did. Remind me to send a bonus to that shopper. You look divine, Zaika moya."

"You don't look so bad yourself," I replied, and really, he didn't.

The man stole my breath from my body. He was gorgeous. That thick chestnut hair was combed back, and his short beard was freshly trimmed. It was the middle of winter, but his skin looked bronzed like he spent hours tanning. Like some golden god, he exuded power and authority.

I already knew the tan came from the forty-five minute swim he completed every day after his meticulous workout. His private pool was on the top floor of his triplex penthouse and the roof was made entirely of some kind of specialty glass. Like the window, no one could see inside unless he made it so.

I could only imagine they were incredibly thick and reinforced. Sunlight filtered in through the glass panes, heating the pool and tanning his skin. I couldn't even fathom the cost. Now that I knew his nickname for me meant bunny, I scrunched up my nose whenever he called me that. Two weeks. Just two weeks left. My heart squeezed whenever I started thinking about it. But time did not slow for anyone. Not even billionaires.

Fact was, the clock was running out on us, on this crazy torrid affair we were embroiled in. Soon my only taste of Adrik would be what I read about in the tabloids. The thought left a bitter taste in my mouth. I didn't want to think about it. The possibility of seeing him in a tabloid with some society princess draped over his arm like a perfect, thin swatch of silk. My heart wouldn't be able to take it.

Stupid, I knew it, but I had feelings for the man. Real ones. I was not from his world. Sure, I knew about the scandals and the marriages, both the loveless and the open kind that seemed to run rampant among the elite. Poor people didn't have the same choices. But the rich seemed to live in a world where bodies were cheap. I couldn't fathom behaving that way.

Adrik seemed different, but what did I really know? Even with all the digging I'd done and the minor facts he'd told me about his life, I still did not know him. Not really. His was a vicious, cruel world, where playing games could sometimes cost lives, or worse, hearts. I said worse because some lives got the end they deserved. A man like Adrik could not afford to form a real connection with anyone. And to soft hearts like mine, that kind of detachment was detrimental.

Working for Missy Castle for six months had taught me a lot about high society life, and if that was really Adrik's world, then the likelihood of me running into him after this was over was slim to none. After all, Missy had fired me, and I did not run in those circles.

My heart squeezed thinking of the time when I wouldn't be able to see him, smell his spicy cologne, or feel his powerful body moving inside of me, bringing me to a completion so strong I passed out once or twice from it. Only Adrik Volkov could possibly command that kind of response from a woman. He was certainly the only man who'd ever done that to me.

Shit. I was falling in love with him. Awareness filled me and I gasped as I darted my gaze to his handsome face, bathed in moonlight seeping in from the windows.

"Zaika? Are you feeling all right?"

"Oh, I'm fine. Sorry. Um, did you know that a Dutchman named Peter Minuit bought the Island of Manhattan in the 17th Century for what was about $24 worth of beads?" I asked, rattling off a factoid I'd recently discovered.

"$24? That was a steal," Adrik observed, his grin quirking one corner of his mouth up in a rakishly adorable expression.

"Yeah. He was a total crook. Native people didn't

share the Europeans concept of ownership, so it was likely a huge misunderstanding," I said, dropping my voice.

"I love that you know so many things, Zaika. You are the most interesting woman I have ever met," he said, flashing me a smile I could only credit as proud.

He took my hand and lifted it to his lips, dropping a kiss on my palm that made my heart pound. His phone vibrated, and he took it out of his pocket with his free hand, still holding mine with the other. It was so big and warm wrapped around mine. I loved the feel of the calluses beneath my fingertips.

Shit. I bit my lip, stifling the gasp that almost slipped free. It was too late, I realized. Too late and I couldn't do a thing about it. Denial wasn't an option, at least not when I was thinking to myself. I didn't know about anyone else, I only knew how I felt. Sex without feelings could not be this intense. There could only be one reason my body lit up like the fourth of July for Adrik and only Adrik. One reason I still refused to allow myself to sleep by his side.

Self-preservation.

That was the real reason. It was too late to guard my heart. But I could try to control how bad it would be for me afterwards. See, I was falling in love with him. Stupid, stupid me cared about the billionaire who'd actually bought me for a month. I shouldn't feel that way. I knew it was dumb, but what could I do? It was too late. And when this was over, when he was gone, it was going to break me.

"How long till we get there?" I asked Adrik even though he was still on the phone.

He covered the receiver with his hand and turned it to look at the time,

"Five minutes, Zaika moya."

I nodded, faked a smile, and casually slid my hand out of his, picking up my clutch instead. I turned my head to the window on the other side of me, trying for composure. But my heart was trying to beat me to death, and I couldn't help the riot of emotions filling me. He was dressed up like some dark prince out of a fairytale, and I matched him like this. My outfit, my hair, but it was only temporary. And that was the part that broke my heart.

Fuck.

How did this happen? We had a routine dammit, and I thought it was working. Every morning, I worked on my book. In the afternoons, I either used his pool or the incredible entertainment system he owned. I was a classic movie junkie, and Adrik had them all. I'd started waiting for him in the nude at first as a sort of surprise. I always wanted to do that thing where the woman wears an apron while serving dinner and nothing else save maybe high heels.

It went so well it became our thing. Sometimes, he came out of the elevator, his shirt, and pants already off. We'd fall into each other, a tangle of arms and legs, sweat and arousal coating our skin as we fucked on every surface of that penthouse. Every day was exciting, every encounter made me want him more. I thought we were growing closer, but my refusal to sleep beside him was still a point of contention. Still, every morning when he left, I could not wait to see him again, and I missed him the moment he was gone.

But the book, well, that was coming along fine. What had started as a sort of tell all about high society was now a full on romantic suspense where the hero was a former underworld crime boss and the heroine an unsuspecting schoolteacher. It might have sounded cliché, but it was moving and gritty. Worlds apart and yet drawn together by an intense desire neither had felt.

Fuck you for thinking it mirrored my reality too closely.

No, really, though, what could I say?

If I was going to have to leave Adrik behind, at

least I could have the fictional version of him to remember. Nothing we really said or did with each other made it to the pages, but the feelings I had, they were right there with my heroine as she fell in love with the one man in the world she could never have.

Adrik finished his call with a soft Russian curse, but the second he tucked his phone away in his inside breast pocket his demeanor changed. His black eyes raked me from head to toe and before I knew it, he'd tugged me back to his side and slammed his mouth to mine with a possessive kiss that I knew had just ruined my carefully applied lipstick.

"There," he growled as the driver stopped and one of his men opened the door. "Now you look claimed."

"What?" I asked, eyes wide, pulse hammering rapidly.

"You looked perfect before, Zaika. But now you look kissed. And kissed is claimed. If another man looks at you tonight for more than the two seconds it takes to realize you belong to someone else, I won't be responsible for what I do to him."

His nostrils flared and the hand that had been stroking my neck tightened with the last word to leave his lips. Then he was gone, standing outside the door with his hand extended for me to grab. I knew there was something really wrong with his statement, that I should not be turned on by his alphahole tendencies. But I was.

I guess maybe it was more than just my clothes that matched the sexy ex-criminal billionaire. Maybe my soul matched his as well. I bit my lips, allowing him to lead me to the entrance of Matthew Castle's Long Island mansion. Why hadn't I known we were going back to this place?

I hated the memory of the last time we were there, the one with Adrik wrapped around some skinny woman on the dancefloor, that flashed through my brain. I stumbled, but his firm hand around my waist steadied me, and he looked down, concern in his dark eyes.

"I swear, Zaika moya, I will touch no one else but you tonight," he whispered in my ear, and chills danced up my spine.

Being so needy and clingy was hardly in my nature, but something happened in the last few days and though I'd tried to hide it from him, he was clearly feeling the same. Possessive instincts were pretty powerful stuff and if the way he glowered at the men taking invitations and standing guard at the entrance of the party was anything to go by, Adrik was having a hard time controlling himself as well.

His face was passive, but his arm contracted several times around me as we walked the perimeter of the ballroom. I got the impression Adrik would rather be anywhere but inside the opulent mansion with throngs of people drinking, shmoozing, and doing God knew what in the dark corners and shadows of the enormous angular room.

There was bass thumping music blasting and a DJ booth set up, special effects lighting flashed all around us, making the ballroom look even more like a Manhattan nightclub than it had last time. Women in haute couture gowns clung to wealthy men like second skins, writhing together as the waitstaff walked by carrying flutes of champagne and other drinks.

I saw people doing drugs right there and frowned. I knew Matthew Castle was a bit of a weasel from things his sister had let slip, and I felt bad for not even checking in on Missy since she fired me. It was stupid of me, really. The woman had let me go without a second glance, and for some reason, I was the one who felt guilty for not checking in.

"Excuse me," a shrill voice said, and I jostled as someone bumped into me.

My eyes widened as I saw the barely dressed woman basically push me out of the way so she could land up against Adrik's chest. But instead, she wound up being caught by Marat at the last minute. How his brother had snuck up on us, I did not know. But I was grateful as Adrik pulled me closer, the frown on his face deepening by the second.

"That was a close call, darling. Maybe lay off the drinks until you learn to walk in those things," Marat said, pointing to her six-inch heels.

He was so handsome, the woman didn't seem to mind. Leaning closer, I heard her practically purring in his ear.

"Ah, the younger Volkov. Well, if I can't have the wolf, the pup will do," she said, wrapping her red-clawed hands around his neck.

"Another time, perhaps. I am afraid I must catch up with my brother," Marat replied, removing her hands from his body, and stepping back.

I watched as emotions I didn't think he had crossed Marat's face. Anger and repugnance were the most prominent. I felt bad. It must have been hard being called a pup, and Adrik's body vibrated with what I recognized was that humming growl he made when angered. I couldn't hear it because of the noise, but he was obviously upset. I pressed my hand to his chest and moved my body closer, wanting to comfort him.

"You okay?" I asked Marat, feeling Adrik's eyes on me while I addressed his brother.

"Of course I am. Brother, I hope you don't mind me saying, but you look beautiful tonight, Sofia," Marat said, slipping his casual playboy mask back on.

"I don't mind if you compliment her, as long as it's in front of me. Besides, she does look beautiful," Adrik agreed, lowering his gaze to my breasts, and squeezing my waist.

"Standing right here, guys," I muttered, feeling my cheeks burn as they spoke about me like I wasn't even there.

Marat smirked, and I rolled my eyes. The ass. I was starting to think of him as an annoyance, but I knew Adrik loved him so I supposed kicking him in the shin would be wrong. We stood together a little while, before I noticed Marat's gaze sharpen on something or someone across the room.

"He's here," he said to Adrik.

"Fine," he growled, turning to me. "I must talk to

our host alone for a few minutes, but Marat will watch out for you while I am gone. Okay?"

"Sure, but I am okay alone," I said, not wanting to stir up any lingering feelings he might have about me and his brother no matter how misguided.

I did not want Marat. Not in the slightest.

"Not tonight, Zaika. This deal has brought out some unsavory characters and I need you protected at all times. My brother will watch you."

And that was that I supposed. He leaned down to kiss me, and it was the first time in my life a man did something like that in public. Tipping my head back, he captured me by the neck and face, laying claim to my mouth and completely ruining me for any other man ever. By the time he lifted his head, his obsidian eyes flashed, and he ran his thumb over my bottom lip, tugging it slightly.

"When I come back, we are leaving and I am going to fuck this mouth, make it mine. Say yes, Zaika," he growled low enough for my ears only.

My body sizzled. I felt my nipples harden beneath the dress and my panties absolutely soaked by my sudden and heady arousal. I nodded my head, but Adrik would not be persuaded to let go of my lower lip until he heard me agree verbally, so I did.

"Yes," I replied, heat filling my vision as I stared up at him.

His smoldering gaze was nearly my undoing, but somehow, I managed to stand there and not turn into a puddle of goo. He turned around quickly and walked across the room to where Matthew Castle stood with his sister, Missy. She was staring right at us, and the look that crossed her face was something I had never seen on the flighty woman before. She looked positively green with envy. That wasn't a look I usually got from other women, especially not wealthy women like Missy.

Why would she be jealous of me? Oh, because of Adrik. Duh. Too bad she didn't know he was only with me because of the fucked up arrangement we had. He wasn't in love with me. He didn't want me for keeps. And knowing that almost sent me to my knees every time I thought it.

"What has you so pensive, little Sofia?" Marat asked, snagging a flute of champagne from a passing server, and handing it to me.

"Oh, nothing. Just my ex-boss is glaring at me from over there," I replied, motioning towards where Adrik was standing talking to Matthew.

"Missy? Yes, well, she's had her eye on Adrik for a long time now," Marat replied and shrugged.

"She has? I worked for her for months, and I never heard her mention him," I said, stunned to hear the news.

"Yes, well, she made the mistake of thinking Adrik liked women who played hard to get. She simply did not understand he did not want her. Period."

"Really?" I said, stunned.

Missy was spoiled, but she was beautiful. I'd never known her to play anything or anyone long-term. Like most of the elite, she thought life was a game with a running score. To Missy, it all depended on how many likes she had or comments to determine whether or not she'd won. Was it wrong I was glad she hadn't won in this case? Maybe. But that was the selfish part of me that wanted to keep Adrik. The childish part that secretly believed it was possible for the ex-crime lord to love me.

Foolish little girl.

"You know," Marat started, looking pensive as he leaned down to talk to me. "I have been digging into Matthew Castle. Both Adrik and I, but we can't find a single reason why he is withholding the sale of CoreTech. He needs the money. Castle Corps is practically drowning in debt," he said, and I wondered why he was talking to me about it.

I knew nothing of that kind of business or finance or any of it. So, I shrugged and replied with the one connection he might have been trying to make.

"I don't know," I said, nibbling my lip. "My job was handling Missy's social calendar. I did not have any direct contact with Matthew except for meetings, and the man gave me the creeps."

"What meetings?" Marat asked.

"Castle Corps meetings and events. Matthew hosts a lot of parties and Missy always attends. Sometimes she required me to go with her. Like the party where I met Adrik," I explained as he led me to a corner away from the dance floor.

"Ah, yes. We've been bombarded with invites lately to parties and dinners. I'd wondered why the infamous Volkov brothers were suddenly on everyone's *must have* lists," he murmured.

"Well, you are both powerful, wealthy, and handsome men. Of course, everyone wants you at their parties," I said, rolling my eyes at him.

"Yes, but not like this. I mean, everyone wants Adrik on their guest list, and I don't have to tell you, he hates parties. Usually they are content to have me," he replied and smirked, pointing to himself as if to say *duh.*

"So you think society's sudden increased interest in Adrik has to do with CoreTech?" I asked.

"I admit, Sof, I really didn't. At least, not until right now. You know, you're really smart," he said, and I shoved him a little. Jerk. Of course, I was smart.

"W-what do you think she wants from Adrik?" I asked, my heart pounding.

"The usual," Marat said, shrugging. "Marriage. Most socialites want to marry a wealthy man so they can continue to live their lavish lifestyles."

I was shocked. Missy never mentioned marriage, but she was always working an angle. When I worked for her, she was extremely meticulous about organizing her social calendar. It was why she wanted an assistant.

"She wants to marry him. She wants to marry the head of Volkov Industries. It would be perfect. Like a fairytale, the Castle princess and the Volkov wolf," I whispered. The idea that the two of them made much more sense than me and him had me stifling a sob. "Would he do that? Marry her to get CoreTech?" I asked before I could stop myself.

Marat's perfectly sculpted brows furrowed, and he shrugged. He was wearing a tailor cut suit, similar to Adrik's. He had all the right looks and was charming and attractive, and so many women stared at him as they passed, it was ridiculous, but I was not moved by any of that. Marat seemed to know it too, and he no longer bothered flirting with me, which was a relief.

"I honestly don't know, Sofia. Adrik was always the one who would do anything to get what he wanted. And I don't say that to upset you. He's told you about our past, yes? Where we came from?" Marat asked, arms crossed as he leaned against the wall.

"A little," I replied.

"Then you understand my brother is ruthless. He will do anything to protect what is his. One moment, I'm sorry, but Josef is calling me. Stay here," Marat said, putting his phone up to his ear.

Marat turned his back towards me, and I stepped back a few feet, needing some space. If Missy wanted Adrik, it was only a matter of time. I'd seen her go after men before. She was beautiful and rich, and she understood these circles much more than I did. I was fooling myself before when I thought Adrik and I were a match, dreaming when I imagined we fit so well together.

Two weeks left, but I didn't think I could go through with it. I couldn't just sit there and pretend I was fine while she made a play for him. Not her. Not him. I groaned as nausea hit me square in the stomach. Marat caught my attention, he was still on the phone.

Are you okay? He mouthed, and I shook my head, pointing towards the ladies' room. He nodded, and I walked off determined to have a quiet minute.

"Where are you running off to, lovey?" someone said in my ear as a wiry arm wrapped around my waist. "I've been looking for you."

A hand clamped over my face before I could respond, and before I knew it, I was being dragged out of the room. It was only a few feet from the corridor, and no one seemed to notice I was being taken somewhere against my will.

My mind immediately went to Adrik, and I tried not to hyperventilate as I was pulled into a dark room. The lights were turned on suddenly, and I blinked hard against the stark brightness.

"Thank you, Charles. Please, sit down, Sofia. I am so glad you could make it," Matthew Castle smirked at me as I was forcibly tossed into a chair by some asshole named Charles.

"W-what are you doing? What do you want?"

"That's easy. I want to know what you told Adrik about me and my sister," he said.

CHAPTER THIRTEEN
ADRIK

I hated leaving Sofia to talk to Matthew Castle in this goddamned house of his. The way he flaunted his family's wealth was distasteful to say the least. I had no love for these parties or these people, but the rumors of Castle Corps increasingly troubled finances, and their impending audit by the Feds, were worrisome. I wanted to get CoreTech under the control of Volkov Industries before the shit could hit the fan.

"Welcome Adrik. Come on, let's go where there is less noise," Matthew said, leading me from the party.

I gritted my teeth as Missy Castle, his sister, walked towards me, claiming my arm in a possessive hold. It took all of my strength not to shake off. I told Zaika moya I would not touch any other women tonight, and while I did not initiate nor return this touch, I did not welcome it.

"Adrik, you look so serious. Maybe your little girlfriend isn't taking such good care of you?" she said, as we entered a flashy office done in golds and maroons.

To me, it looked like something out of a cheesy mafia movie or a bad interpretation of Dracula. But whatever. I did not care how the Castle family decorated their home. I just wanted CoreTech, then I wanted to get back to my Zaika.

"My personal life is not your business, Miss Castle," I said, finally removing her hand from my arm.

She gasped and frowned, hissing angrily as she took the chair behind the desk. I turned to see Matthew had not followed us inside.

"What is this? What do you want?"

"Haven't you figured it out yet, Adrik? Matthew is nothing! He has no real pull anymore," she said and snorted.

I stood frozen as I went over the hundreds of meetings we'd had over the past six months with Matthew Castle over CoreTech. His vague responses to questions. His noncommittal answers. Fuck. How did we miss this?

"What are you saying, exactly?" I asked, refusing to show her any emotion at all.

"I own CoreTech, silly," she said, and batted her eyelashes at me in some horrific caricature of a demure young lady. But Missy was too hard and experienced to pretend that sort of innocence. Not that it would matter. The woman was repulsive to me.

"Okay. Then why would you have us meet with your brother and not you?"

"Well, I was hoping with these parties and dinners you or your brother would have broken down by now and proposed an arrangement that might include more than business. But you Volkov brothers are colder than even your reputation," she explained, and I gritted my teeth.

"Had you simply asked, Missy, I would have told you there will be no merger between us. Not business and not personal. Volkov Industries wants to buy CoreTech. I am willing to pay the market price, but that is all I am offering," I said.

"Well, it's not enough!" she yelled. "Is it her? Is my former assistant the reason you're being so dumb?

It's just pussy, Adrik. You can get that anywhere. Hell! I will even let you keep her. That is if you still want her after my brother is finished—"

Her crazed eyes flashed, and for the first time since I was a child, I felt fear. Not for me. But for Zaika moya. What had this insane female done to my Sofia?

"What did you say?" I asked as fury and fear battled within me.

"I said my brother has her now, and he's probably already left his mark. So, if it is sloppy seconds you want, Adrik, you can have them. *After* we are married and we merge Volkov Industries and Castle Corp," she replied, cackling like a crazy witch.

I normally did not hit women. But I had never been as tempted to before then. I grabbed my phone and called Josef, telling him what was going on and asking for confirmation that Marat had Sofia.

"Where is Sofia?" I asked my head of security.

"She's gone boss. She said she had to go to the restroom, but she never came back—"

"FIND HER!" I bellowed into the phone.

I stalked over to where Missy sat behind the desk and took the chair by the arms, shaking it once, to get her attention. She giggled maniacally, then snapped her jaw shut when she finally looked at me.

"Where did your brother take her?" I asked between gritted teeth, hatred and fury boiling over inside me.

"Wouldn't you like to know," Missy started.

I shoved the chair back to the wall just as some of my guards filed in. One of whom was a woman. I stepped back and pointed to Adelita.

"She has three seconds to tell me where her brother is. If she does not comply, start cutting off her fingers until she does," I said without emotion, even though my heart was beating wildly inside my chest.

If Matthew had hurt her—if he laid one hand on her precious head, I would tear him limb from limb. There was no coming back from this, I did not care how rich he was or how old his family name was. If my Sofia was in any way molested by him, I would wipe the Castles from the face of the earth. Anger filled me and I growled with it.

"No, no, no! Do not touch me!" shrieked Missy.

She looked afraid as Adelita approached dressed in all black, guns and knives holstered to her person. I'd seen her work before, and the woman was a master. I wish I could say I cared what she would do to Missy. But I didn't.

"Fine, fine. I will tell you! Adrik, just stop her and

I will tell you where they are. I can't believe you are getting worked up over Sofia," she said, shaking her head. Stupid woman. "She is nobody! Look, consider my offer first—"

"Adelita," I said, cutting off another insane tirade.

Time was wasting, and I nodded at one of my deadliest security guards as she stepped forward. Adelita was very well trained in martial arts, but her specialty was knives. I did not like to hurt women, but this was the twenty-first century, and I was not a fool.

In fact, I was a feminist. Women made war too. So, I made it my business to have my own female guards so they could handle cases such as this. Adelita grinned, nodding her head before she grabbed Missy by the hair.

"Ahh! He has her down the hall! He has her down the hall! In Daddy's old office. Now, let me go," she whimpered, but it was too late for her.

"On it," Josef said, racing out the door in front of me, Marat on his heels.

"Let me go now. I told you," Missy yelled, but it was too late for her.

"Finish it," I commanded.

Missy Castle should never have fucked with me or mine. I nodded once towards Adelita, giving my permission for her to dole the lesson that woman needed to learn before I joined my head of security and brother in racing out of the room.

A scream followed by a loud blow resounded in the background. A few more and a familiar popping sound followed. But that did not concern me. My team was well-trained and very loyal—that happened when you paid like I did.

They were all handpicked by me. Each had a past, a history that made them unemployable elsewhere. I knew all their secrets and I kept them close. So no, I had no doubts whatsoever that they would do what I commanded.

It took three precious minutes to race down the hall to what was old man Castle's office. Of course, we'd reconned the place before the first time any of us had ever stepped foot inside. A holdover from our criminal enterprise days, but smart, nonetheless. Josef reached the doors first, pulling them open. But I was inside before any of them, and I had that motherfucker by the throat before he could finish whatever he'd been attempting to do.

I turned my head to see Sofia shaking against the wall. Another man had had his hands on hers, holding her back, but Marat and Josef were on him.

"Are you okay?" I asked.

My eyes raked over her face, her body, then back to her tear-stained face. That motherfucker was going to pay. Anger filled me, made my vision red. Sofia gasped. She was shaking, but she nodded, and I noticed a red mark on her face.

"You hit my woman?" I turned slowly as I asked the question.

"No! No! It wasn't me. It was Charles!" Matthew said, gasping and trying to get my fingers off his throat.

"You. Hit. My. Woman."

My voice was guttural and deep, more animal than man. I spoke with my jaw clenched so hard, it was amazing any words came out at all. But I was holding on to control by a thread.

"Adrik, we can work this out—"

I punched him in the gut before he could finish whatever garbage proposal he'd planned on making. Then, I pummeled his face, driving my closed fist into his pasty flesh again and again. Blow after blow, relentlessly, I hit him over and over the crunch of his nose and cheek bones breaking, then his teeth, echoed in the room. Blood spurted as I kept hitting him, but I did not stop. I could not. I hit him over and over again until his face was a bloody pulp, and he was dead weight in my grip.

"Adrik, that's enough," Marat said, grabbing my arm, and I almost hit him, too.

Luckily, I was not too far gone to remember who he was or where I was. The second I dropped what was left of Castle, I moved towards Zaika moya. She crumpled in my arms, sobbing against me.

"Get everyone out of here. Bring him and this soon to be dead motherfucker to the place. No more games. We take over Castle Corps now, tonight. Hostile as fuck," I ordered between gritted teeth.

"Torch it?" Josef asked.

I nodded once, picking Sofia up in my arms and walking out the door to where my car waited. She was shivering uncontrollably, and I knew I should have washed the blood from my hands before touching her, but I could not spare the time. I had to get her home. Not to my penthouse, but to my home. I had to make sure she was safe. Needed to see it with my own eyes.

Murmuring to her in Russian for the duration of the twenty-minute drive to my own estate on the Long Island Sound, I ordered my men to double the guard and make sure we were not disturbed.

"Y-you can put me down. I can walk," she said, but I squeezed her tighter as I took the stairs two at a time.

"Not on your life," I told her.

The front door opened for me, and I barely looked at Esmerelda, my housekeeper before taking off for my bedroom. This was my real home. A modern mansion designed to my specifications. None of that old world opulence, but a sleeker design with built in tech that made this home a veritable fortress. I'd installed biometric security systems and employed armed guards who'd been with me for years.

Once safely ensconced in my bedroom, I carried Sofia to the adjoining bathroom and placed her sitting on the counter. Turning around, I started the bath, adding some salts and other fancy shit I'd never used. She watched me, her huge velvet eyes big in her pale face, and fuck, I wanted to kill him all over again.

I washed my hands in the sink, not even noticing the blood that circled the drain before I removed my jacket and shirt. I wore just an undershirt and my pants when I turned back to her.

"Come, Zaika," I murmured, helping her to stand.

She allowed me to undress her, and I wanted to roar like a wounded beast at the marks they had left on her perfect skin. It was clear she had been slapped across the face. But it was the handprints on her wrist that infuriated me. I knew Josef and Marat would hold that fucker, the man named Charles, for me. And I could not wait to get my hands on him. But that would be later. After I made sure she was okay.

"I'm okay," she said, wincing a little when she tried to smile.

"I should never have left you. I am so sorry," I said, barely able to contain my agony as I tried to apologize.

"It was only one slap—"

"One slap is too many. It should never have happened. I failed to keep you safe, but I swear I will never do that again."

"You won't have to," she said, turning away from me as she stepped into the tub, fully naked now.

"What do you mean?"

"This is only temporary, right? Two weeks left, Adrik, then I'll be out of your life, unless you want me gone soon—"

That was as far as I allowed her to get before I followed her into the tub, pants, and everything. I grabbed her roughly, too roughly, and crashed my lips to hers. Overcome with the need to show her exactly who I was, and who she belonged to. Oh, my Zaika was playing with fire.

Taunting me about how little time we had left. Maybe it was the nights she refused to sleep beside me. Or the threat to her that had happened because of me. Whatever spurned me on, I was a rutting animal. My hands clutched at her body as I plundered her mouth with my own.

"You are not going anywhere. You belong to me," I growled, digging my fingers into her hips as I unzipped my pants and pushed them down my legs.

I didn't give a shit about the fact the wool was now soaked in bathwater and likely ruined. Her hands were on me, tugging at the undershirt I had on, and I let her slide it over my head. The slapping sounds our wet bodies made were symphonic in the marble bathroom. The tub was full of steaming water, and I sat down, pulling her astride me.

"You're so fucking wet for me," I growled as I slid a hand between us and pushed two fingers into her sweet slit.

I cupped her neck with one hand, shoving my tongue into her mouth, mimicking the way I was fucking her on my hand. She moaned, and it was so damn sexy. My cock was so hard, I could probably hammer a nail with it. But I wasn't about to sink into her yet, not until she came at least once by my fingers.

"Why?" she asked me when I finally let her up for air.

"Why what? Why fuck this pussy with my fingers? Cause I want to feel it ripple around me when you come screaming my name," I told her, and her velvet eyes turned molten. Her sex squeezed my fingers, and I knew she was close as she rocked against me, searching for her pleasure.

"No, why did you do that to him?"

"You want to talk about that now? While I fuck you with my fingers?" I growled against her neck.

I sucked the spot that always seemed to make her squirm and was rewarded with another squeeze of my fingers. Close now. She was so close. And I needed her to come, so I could finally fill her with my cock.

"Because you're mine."

"For two weeks," she said.

"Does not matter how long," I growled, suddenly angry at the reminder of the time constraints I so stupidly put on our relationship. "You are mine right now. No one touches what is mine. Understand? Anyone touches you, I will kill them," I said, and fuck, she must have liked that because she started to come.

Water sloshed over the side of the tub as her pussy squeezed around my fingers, and Sofia loosed a guttural moan that echoed in the bathroom. She was panting, but I did not allow her any time to come down. I lifted her by her hips and slammed her down on my cock. So far gone, I hadn't even considered a condom or anything except the relief I felt, the purely profound fucking joy of being buried balls deep inside her.

"Look at how good you take all of me, Zaika moya. So fucking perfect. Soft, hot, wet, you feel like heaven," I growled against her tight nipple, sucking it into my mouth as I bounced her up and down on my cock.

"Tell me you're mine," I demanded, pumping my hips as I lifted and slammed her up, down, harder, faster. "Tell me!" I snarled, more beast than man.

"I'm yours. I'm yours. Fuck, Adrik, I'm gonna come again," she said, and I groaned, already feeling the ripples of her pussy fluttering around me.

My cock swelled even more as she tightened her grip, her pussy squeezing me harder than ever. Just as she fell over the edge, I felt my whole world tilt on its axis and pleasure the likes of which I had never felt before filled me as I erupted inside her like a long dormant volcano.

My chest rumbled in deep satisfaction when I plucked her off me and got out of the tub, grabbing a towel to wrap around my waist, and another for her, I lifted Zaika moya from the now cool water, and carried her to the bed. It did not matter that I'd just had her, and she'd already come twice for me. I needed her to come again.

I was manic with my need to touch her, kiss her, possess her. It was a complete and total compulsion. Like I could never possibly be whole until I had her coming on every part of me. My tongue was next, and I must have said it aloud if her squeak when I dropped her on the bed was anything to go by.

Water droplets dotted her perfect porcelain skin, and the breath swooshed from my lungs. She was so beautiful. Sable hair hung in wet tendrils down her shoulders, making rivers of water flood down the valley between her big tits. Fuck, she was so perfect, her velvet eyes were keen on me as I watched her, memorizing her with my eyes.

But it wasn't enough. Breathing heavily, I ran my palms down her front, cupping her tits, tweaking the nipples, and sliding lower to her soft belly, wide hips, and thick thighs.

"Adrik," she moaned. "Please."

"Please what?"

"Please, touch me."

"I am touching you, Zaika."

"More," she begged. "I need more."

I kneeled before her, naked as she was and parted her thighs. Her pussy was pink and swollen with need, glistening before me like the most delicious feast I had ever seen. I licked my lips, ready to worship at my goddess' altar. This woman owned me. She held pieces of my soul in the palm of her hands, and it should have terrified me that she had such control. But she did not know it yet. And I was too far gone for confessions.

"Mine," I growled before closing my mouth over her tiny swollen clit.

Sofia bucked wildly against me, and I was forced to hold her down with one arm across her hips. Fuck, she tasted like ambrosia. Nothing compared to her sweet honey, and I sucked it all down, greedy for every last drop. Heat filled my chest and raw possession pummeled through me, fucking me up for every other emotion.

Sofia had been taken from me that night. This fucking world I lived in. Corporations and high rises. These people were criminals just like the thugs who once thought to prey on me and my brother on the cold streets of Moscow. But I was the Dark Wolf. I would pay them back tenfold for the affront of trying to take what was mine.

And. She. Was. Mine.

CHAPTER FOURTEEN
SOFIA

"Tell me," Adrik whispered as he cradled me in his arms.

I closed my eyes, snuggling against his chest. I did not want to talk about what had happened earlier that night. Didn't want to remember how scared I'd been or angry at Missy, at myself, for what that crazy bitch had done. I knew rich people could be selfish, but what she'd tried to do was truly heinous.

No, I did not want to remember, but after the way Adrik had come for me. Like some dark avenging angel, I couldn't deny him anything. So, if he wanted those words from me, I would give them to him. I would give anything to him.

"Matthew had his man, *Charles*, grab me from the

party. I'd left Marat to use the restroom, and he was stealthy about it. It wasn't Marat's fault," I said, rubbing Adrik's chest when he started to rumble.

"He brought me to an office and inside, Matthew Castle waited. H-he held me by the wrists, said he was going to show you that no one could tell him what to do. He tried to kiss me, but I head-butted him, so he slapped me instead. And that was when you came in," I finished.

"I am so fucking sorry, Sofia," he grunted, and I closed my eyes on a wave of hurt. I didn't want him to call me by name. I wanted to be his Zaika again.

Did he see me differently now? Would he push me away?

I didn't know how a man like Adrik would react to such an attack on his power and strength. Maybe he would hate me now. Maybe I would be a reminder of how he was momentarily blindsided.

"Thank you," I whispered, pressing my lips to his chest. "Thank you for coming for me, for what you did to him. Thank you, thank you," I repeated myself, kissing him over and over again as tears leaked from my eyes.

Before Adrik left me, before our time was up, I had to make sure he understood. I had to make sure he knew how much that meant to me having him on my side. Protecting me when someone powerful like Matthew could have so easily done whatever it was he wanted to do to someone like me, and likely he would have gotten away with it. But Adrik had stopped him. And I owed him everything.

"Hey, hey, what is this? You're thanking me for letting you get taken? For beating a man to death in front of you?"

"No! I am thanking you for making me feel safe," I tried to explain.

"What are you talking about? I fucking failed," he growled, and I knew he was angry at himself.

"No, Adrik, you didn't. I am right here, and I am okay, and that is because of you. Only you. You protected me. You did," I said and pressed my mouth to his.

He froze beneath me for a full thirty seconds, and I thought for sure that was it. He was going to shove me off him and order me to leave. But he didn't. Instead, I felt his arms wrap around me like steel bands as he pulled me on top of him.

His body was hard and hot and so damn safe. Even after everything, his arms offered the most security I had ever felt in my life. His spicy scent filled my nostrils, and I wanted to rub myself all over him. Everywhere, every inch. I wanted to roll around in it until it became a part of me. God, what would that be like? To carry his scent on my skin every single day? I could only dream about such things. But for tonight, for now, I could have this. I could have him all night long if I wanted. And I did want.

Adrik grunted beneath me, and I didn't know if it was my weight or the feel of my slick pussy, which seems to be constantly wet when I was near him, sliding over his hardened shaft. His dick is so thick and girthy, it hit my clit just right as I slid up and down, flexing my hips.

"I didn't use a condom either time tonight," he growled, and I stopped moving.

Then I grinned, cupping his cheeks, and kissing him again. Hard, deep, thrusting my tongue into his mouth as I fit his cock to my entrance and take him all the way inside.

"I have an IUD. I've been on birth control since I was eighteen to regulate my menstrual cycle."

I gasped after I said the last words and he flexed his hips, sitting up and dragging his mouth over my breasts to suck on my swollen nipples. He was so hard, I felt him stretch my walls and though we'd already had sex twice that night, this time, he felt bigger.

"Now, you tell me this, Zaika? Why not before? Do you know how badly I want to fuck you raw," he grunts, and his accent was thicker with his arousal.

"Please," I begged, wanting it as much as he did.

I loved the fact that nothing separated us now. His dick felt so good, so perfect, and every time he flexed, he stroked along my g-spot, sending spirals of pleasure rocketing through me. I was trapped between the hard bars of his arms and his dick. He held me there, impaled on him as he flexed in shallow thrusts, rubbing my clit until my orgasm hit me hard and fast. Then the world flipped over, or maybe that was just me. I was on my back suddenly, legs over his shoulders as he pounded into me, making the enormous four-poster bed we were on shake with every thrust.

Adrik roared when he came, clamping his teeth around my shoulder as his cock throbbed inside me. My legs shook, I was coming again, spurred on by the sensation of his hot ropes of cum filling my core. Fuck, it felt so good. So right.

For a moment, dark thoughts filled me. I wished I didn't have that IUD. That I'd get pregnant by him. But that was a silly girl's fantasy. A foolish whim. I would never trap him like that. Someday, I would get married and have children and they would be loved.

But they would be made knowingly, not by mistake or for any other reason than because me and their father wanted them.

Tears pricked my eyes because I wished that father would be Adrik. But we only had two weeks left. And that was highly unlikely.

"Stay," he growled the word as he slid out of my sheath. Just that word. Just stay. The same plea he made almost every time we fucked.

The difference was after everything that had happened earlier tonight, I couldn't say no. It was physically impossible for me to even utter that word if I tried. And I didn't want to try. I was tired of denying him, denying us. I wanted to feel him around me all night. I wanted to stay by his side, in his bed, until the sun came up.

"Yes, Adrik. I'll stay," I whispered, feeling him tense above me.

"Say it again."

"I'll stay."

"You will stay?"

"Yes."

"Again," he demanded. "Say it again, Zaika moya."

"I'll stay with you. In your bed. In your arms. All. Night. Long."

His chest rumbled, and moisture flooded

between my legs. No one had ever had that effect on me. Only Adrik could conjure my arousal like a wizard casting a spell with magic words. God, he was so handsome. So big. So everything.

"One more time, Sofia."

"I'll stay," I repeated, willing to say it a hundred times if he wanted me to.

Then he cupped my face with his hand, stroking my neck and shoulders before dipping his head to kiss me sweetly. Those tears I'd tried to keep at bay won the battle, rolling down my cheeks and making their way into our kiss.

"Shhh, Zaika moya," he whispered, kissing my face, licking away my tears. A stream of Russian fell from his lips, and I couldn't understand what he was saying, but I didn't care. His tone was comforting, and he held me close against his hard, warm body.

Never in my life had I felt so protected, so safe, and cared for. Even if it was only temporary.

The next morning, I woke up alone. The sound of waves crashing on the shore was distant, but it stirred me. I got out of the enormous bed, running my hands over the impossibly soft sheets and blanket. The entire bedroom was done in blacks and grays, and I smiled. It was very much like his penthouse in the city, and I thought he must have used the same designer.

Everything was so masculine. Wood, metal, glass. The tones were cool and the artwork on the walls impersonal. The black marble bathroom was incredible, and I was pleased to see a new toothbrush waiting for me by the sink. I nearly screamed when I got a look at myself. My hair was sticking up and my makeup from the night before was smudged beneath my eyes.

I indulged myself with a hot shower from his twelve headed shower stall. Holy fuck. If this was what you could afford when you made a billion dollars, I could not understand why more people weren't out there busting their asses. It was fucking sublime. I exited the shower, grabbed a fluffy robe from the heated rack, and wrapped it around my thoroughly relaxed body.

Next, I shuffled through his drawers and cabinets, hoping to find deodorant and lotion, but hoping even more to not find anything that was for women. My prayers were answered, and I grinned as I used his utterly masculine toiletries. Clothes were going to be a problem, I thought as I brushed my hair and used some extra conditioner since I didn't have any of my products there either and his man goop simply would not cut it.

I went back to the bedroom and was surprised when I saw a couple of shopping bags containing some lingerie, soft, expensive leggings, and even softer sweaters to top them with. My face hurt from smiling, but I couldn't stop that either. Especially not when I found a pair of furry gray UGG slippers at the bottom of one of the bags.

My stomach was growling by the time I was dressed, and I left the bedroom, hoping to find Adrik. I had mixed feelings about this morning since I'd finally stayed the night with him, and he hadn't been there in the morning. Was he tired of me already? Had it been all about the chase? I gnawed on my lower lip and followed the scent of food to the kitchen downstairs.

There was an informal dining room off the main living room area and a small buffet had been set up with chafing dishes. I closed my eyes as I inhaled and opened them again to find Marat grinning at an older woman who was carrying a tray of coffee.

"Oh, Mr. Volkov, you are such a flirt," the older woman said and giggled as he took the tray from her and kissed her weathered cheek.

"You wound me, fair lady! Come now, you know

you are my best girl, Rosa," he told her with false sincerity.

She seemed to know all about him and his shenanigans, and whacked him with her tea towel for his efforts. Good for her. Her eyes flashed to mine, and she nodded nervously. I smiled at her, and she blinked before smiling back.

"Oh, this one is polite. Not like the others," she whispered to Marat, but I could still hear her.

"Good morning, or should I say, afternoon, Sofia. Rosa, this one is Adrik's, not mine," Marat corrected her, and relief filled me.

I didn't want to be just another one night stand. Even if I kinda sorta was. Shit. When this was over, it was going to crush me. But even knowing it, I couldn't stop myself from wanting him and needing him. Speaking of which.

"Is Adrik here?" I asked, but Marat's face clouded over.

"Sit down. Let's eat," he said, and I wanted to refuse, but my stomach was growling.

I made a plate, joining Marat at the table. He looked worried and kept his phone next to his cup of coffee.

"Adrik is gone. He had to leave the country," he started.

"What?"

"There was a problem at one of our mines, and he needed to go in person to take care of it. He got the call very early, Sofia, but he did not want to wake you."

"When will he be back?" I asked.

"I don't know. These things depend on a lot of different moving parts. There are government officials involved, corporate enemies."

"Geez. The business world seems every bit as cutthroat as the criminal world," I murmured and covered my mouth with one hand.

"Ha! You might be right. Going legit was not as difficult a transition as one might think. And yes, the powerful operate very much like the mafia," Marat confided with a frankness I hadn't expected.

"I don't, I mean, I can't stay here without him," I said, wiping my mouth after I finished eating.

"Sofia, no. I'm sorry, but he won't want you to leave," Marat replied.

"You can't keep me here. And since we don't know when he will return, I don't feel right."

"Just wait a few days, okay? Let's wait to hear from him at least. Will you do that?"

I nodded my head and stood up, like the weak person I'd somehow become. I was hurt that he hadn't bothered to wake me to say goodbye, and I was desperate for some kind of confirmation that what we shared wasn't something I'd just imagined. Was it just fate that took him from me the one night I said yes and stayed? Or was it an excuse?

Marat had some people go to the penthouse to collect my things, but all I really wanted was my laptop. Still, it was nice to have clothes and my skin care regime with me. February was bitterly cold.

All the forced heat made my skin dry, but that was nothing compared to how hollow my heart felt. I stared at my cell phone, waiting for a reply I knew was not coming.

Day One

SOFIA

Adrik? Marat gave me your number.
Can you give me an update?

Day Two

SOFIA

I'm still here. Waiting.

Day Three

SOFIA

I miss you. Can you call or text, so I
know you are safe?

A few days later, there was still no word from Adrik. At least, not for me. I called Nonna and surprisingly my Dad answered.

"Hello? That you, baby butterfly?" Dad asked, his familiar voice sifting through the phone, and I closed my eyes. It had been years since he'd called me that.

"Dad? What are you doing?"

"I'm helping Nonna with some repairs to the kitchen. You know, she's been wanting new cabinets forever."

"You are?" I asked completely shocked.

"Yeah, yeah. You know, I've been getting help. Stopped drinking. Got one of those sponsors," he said, and I couldn't believe it.

"Oh my God, Dad, that is amazing."

"Nah. It was long overdue. Anyway, thank that fella of yours. Maybe you both come down for lunch the Sunday after next? I should have the cabinets done before then," he said.

"W-what does Adrik have to do with it?" I asked.

My pulse was going crazy and my heart was pounding as my father, who hadn't been sober since my mother was alive for more than a few hours, explained that Adrik hired a building manager for Nonna, as well as a crew to fix all the construction issues. The manager, an older man named Vince, moved into the basement apartment with his wife, Trudy, right after our visit.

Vince had been working on getting every one of my aunts, uncles, and cousins on a payment plan to bring them up to current with their past due rents, while collecting the regular monthly rent and utilities Nonna charged them, which was not much at all, but those fuckers thought family meant free. Apparently, Vince was a hardass, but he was nice and Trudy and Nonna had become fast friends.

"Uncle Frank is gone, and Aunt Linda is so much happier without that douche. I'm so sorry about how he treated you, Sofia. I wasn't right in the head, and I wasn't there for you. I am so sorry. Your mother would have wanted me to take better care of you," he gasped, sniffing, and I knew he was crying.

"It's okay, Daddy. You did what you could, and Nonna was there for me," I said, forgiving him for everything on the spot.

"You know, Aunt Linda comes with me to AA, too. She takes Nonna to church now and uh, she's got a job at the corner store," Dad said, and by that point I was crying, too.

"I am so happy, Dad. And uh, yeah, I'll be over Sunday," I said, skating over the fact Adrik was gone and I didn't know how long would pass until I heard from him again.

The next week passed by slowly. We had a nor'easter that brought with it twelve inches of snow, and Long Island got hit particularly hard. By the time the next Sunday rolled around, the streets had been cleared, and I was missing Adrik so badly, I didn't know what to do.

I knew he called and spoke with Marat. But he never asked for me, and he didn't return any of the texts I had sent him. So on that Sunday I was supposed to go to Nonna's I made a deal with myself. I was going to stay there. Start my life over without him and chalk it up to some crazy fantasy that had happened.

"What are you doing? Where do you think you are going?" Marat asked.

He frowned when he saw me dressed in one of the outfits Adrik's people had taken from my apartment weeks ago. But there was just no way I was taking any of that other stuff.

"You asked me to wait, but we both know I don't belong here, Marat. Adrik hasn't spoken to me since he left, and I don't want to wait for him to come back to leave. It will be too hard," I whispered, my voice breaking at the end.

"He'll kill me if I let you go," Marat said, but I could tell he was leaning towards doing it.

"He won't. We both know I was just a passing thing. This is better for him. Clean," I said, and shrugged.

"Holy fuck. You love him!"

"Oh, God, Marat! Just, you can have someone drive me to my grandmother's place, okay? You can tell him I got there safely. He won't be mad. I-I can't stay here. Please!" I yelled back, and by then I was sobbing.

"Shit. Okay, okay, come here, it's okay," Marat said, and side-hugged me awkwardly. It was more of a side-pat on the shoulders really before he pushed me away and handed me a silk handkerchief. I blew my nose in it and attempted to hand it back, but he shook his head.

"Um, you can keep that one, Sof," he said, and grabbed my bag from my hands.

I laughed, wiping my tears as we went. The ride to Jersey was long. That was to be expected what with all the snow and people driving like shit. You would think New Yorkers and New Jersey folks would be used to it, but nope. Accidents littered the highway, and I was glad Marat seemed an expert behind the wheel of the enormous SUV. He'd insisted on driving me himself, though I noticed a similar SUV driving behind us with a group of hard looking men I recognized as being part of their security team.

When we finally arrived, I hesitated, but steeled myself, opening the door.

"You don't have to go, Sofia. Come back to the house. Adrik will come to his senses," Marat said.

"Nah. I know better than to stay someplace I never should have been, anyway. Your brother was beautiful to me."

"He doesn't know love. Never had it. Understand? He was always bound to fuck it up. But you can help him," Marat implored.

"He doesn't need me to help him. He's the Dark Wolf. He can do anything," I said, believing that with all my heart.

"He told you that name?" Marat asked, head cocked to the side.

"Yeah."

"And you didn't run screaming?"

"No. Why would I?"

"And after what he did to that prick at the party?"

"What about it? That bastard deserved what he got," I said, and I meant it.

I told Adrik that night what Matthew had done

to me, but I didn't tell him what he said he was going to do or how he bragged about raping and hurting women before. Said it was the privilege of his class. No, I was not upset about Adrik's actions. Fuck, I applauded them.

"You know, the other man, Charles, he got worse," Marat said, watching me closely.

"Good," I replied and got out of the truck.

"My brother is an idiot," Marat said, shaking his head.

"Ha! I dare you to say that to his face."

"No, thank you. I am not an idiot," he replied with a wink, and watched me walk up the stairs.

I waved him off and went inside. I didn't know how I was going to live after everything I'd been through. But I had to try. I already missed him like crazy. But if he wanted me, he would've answered my texts. Would have tried to call. But he didn't, so there I was, broken heart and ruined soul, a shell of my former self.

If only he loved me back. If only I hadn't stayed that night.

If only...

CHAPTER FIFTEEN
ADRIK

Before my private plane even touched the ground, I was unbuckled and waiting at the door. Ten days. I'd spent ten days across the world from Zaika moya and I felt like a caged animal.

I knew I should have called. I stared at the texts she'd written me while I was gone and frowned heavily at the last one. It was dated two days ago.

SOFIA

It's been eight days since you left, I pray you are safe, and Marat assures me you are. I wasn't going to text you anymore, but I didn't want you to think I was a coward. And I didn't want to leave without saying goodbye. Thank you for everything.

P.S. I told you staying was a mistake.

She was gone. Zaika moya had left my home, my life, just like that. She could not even wait for me to get back to say it to my face. Anger and rage and disbelief coursed through me, and I felt like a wild thing. That last line, though. That P.S. at the end, that was the killer. That was the bullet straight to my heart.

It was that line that had me wanting to jump off this plane and head right to North Bergen where I knew she'd returned from my brother. That asshole had driven her. I warred between applauding his efforts to keep her safe—yes, he had a guard on her night and day without her noticing. And yet, I was still going to punch him in his stupid face.

Sofia was gone. Fuck. She did not take a single thing from my house. Not one of her new outfits or accessories I'd purchased. But she wouldn't, would she? I'd tried to build a cage to put her in, to keep her with me, but she refused to stay trapped. And I needed to know why. I needed to know what I had to do to make her mine forever. Not this fucking one month bullshit I had her promise to give me. And if that failed, I would still drag her back. She owed me four days. I had four fucking days left from our original agreement.

Then I would tie her to the damn bed and fuck her till she was too weak to refuse me anymore. I would have my Zaika. She would be mine. Fuck the state of the country I just left.

Fighting to keep our claims on the rare earth metal mines we had in numerous countries required bribes, fights, and murder. My hands were far from clean, but I would do worse to keep Sofia with me. Before I'd gone to my private jet, the morning I was pulled from the bed we'd shared, I'd had one more thing to do to avenge the woman I was crazy about.

I still could not believe she had finally agreed to stay with me for the entire night. It was everything I wanted and more. The feel of her soft body nestled against mine, seeking comfort from me. The Dark Wolf. As if I were somehow worthy of her. If I closed my eyes, I could still feel her warm breath tickling my skin.

But then, the shit hit the fan, and I had to leave to protect what was ours. But first, I went to the place to avenge her. That was what we called the warehouse we owned just outside the Lincoln Tunnel. Marat met me there with Josef, of course. Matthew

Castle was already dead, his body disposed of, and Missy, well, she was in an unfortunate accident at her home estate. The fire had left her alive, but barely coherent. Poor thing.

Charles Manheim, Matthew's right-hand man, was hanging upside down from a metal hook, blood seeping from his many lacerations onto the cold, concrete floor. I called the cleaners beforehand, letting them know where to come take care of the mess.

They were good at that sort of thing. Getting rid of any trace DNA and disposing of corpses. That was all Charles was at the time. A breathing corpse. But that had changed soon after my arrival.

"Did you get everything we needed?" I asked Marat.

My brother nodded, and Josef had handed me the blade he already had out.

"Normally, I would drag this out for what you did, you piece of shit. You touched what was mine."

"N-no. P-please," he whispered hoarsely.

"Nyet. There is no please for you," I told him, and stood up, slicing his femoral artery with one swipe of the knife through his pants and flesh. *"Let him bleed out. Then Bury him with the rest of the filth."*

"Yes, *boss*," Josef said, his wide grin telling me he would see to the job personally.

He had gotten off lucky. As for the business over-seas. We were back in control, and the people who needed the reminder the Dark Wolf was still afoot got it. Tenfold. But I did not give a fuck for them or any of it. In fact, the whole fucking world could burn for all I cared if I did not have her.

"Adrik! Damn, you look fucked up!" Marat shouted as I raced down the runway after disembarking from the plane.

"Where is she? Is she safe?"

"Yes. She is at her grandmother's. Her father is with her. They are painting," Marat said.

"Painting?"

"Yes. The hallway. Vince reported earlier, she insisted on helping."

I growled and got inside the waiting SUV. Josef was driving and Andres was in the back. I glanced at my assistant, but he was looking down at his tablet. When Marat slid in beside him, he started talking to my brother about business, and I was stunned. Marat was the face of Volkov Industries, but my brother hardly took an interest in things.

"I hope you do not mind, Mr. Volkov, but your brother has been taking care of some of the more pressing matters involving our takeover of Castle

Corp, and more importantly, CoreTech, while you were occupied," Andres explained.

"Is this true Marat?"

At my brother's nod, I grinned. It was about time he stepped up.

"Then it is fine, Andres. You have my complete permission to do anything my brother says, he is half-owner and co-chair of Volkov Industries, you know," I replied.

"I am?" Marat asked.

"For fuck's sake, don't you read anything I make you sign?" I asked exasperated.

Josef snorted, covering his laugh with a cough. We spent the following forty-five minutes discussing business. But then we were there, and I could not put off what was about to happen anymore than I could stop a hurricane or the tide.

I took the stairs to the building two at a time, approving of the way they and the sidewalk were cleared of snow and salted. Couldn't have her grandmother slipping on any slick out there, could we? The smell of fresh paint permeated the air, and I walked down the hall, impatient to see her.

Imagine my shock when I came upon her right outside her grandmother's door wearing a tight pair of leggings and a baggy t-shirt while climbing a ladder. Her hair was in a ponytail, and she had on a cap. Paint was liberally smeared across her clothing and my heart squeezed painfully in my chest. She was so fucking beautiful.

"Adrik!" she squeaked, turning around far too quickly.

The ladder shook, and she started to fall, grabbing onto the top and spilling the gallon of paint onto the floor. It splattered the shit out of me, ruining my shoes and suit. But I did not give two fucks. I grabbed her before she could follow it down, pulling her into my arms and crushing her soft weight against my chest.

"You have a lot of explaining to do, Zaika moya," I growled, kissing her desperately before she could respond.

I backed her up against the wall, not caring about the wet paint or the fact we had an audience. I just kissed her, and kissed her, and kissed her some more.

"Um, Sof? Are you okay?" a man asked.

I looked up ready to fight, but it was her father. So, I nodded and allowed her to slide down my body till her feet hit the floor.

"Oh, um, yeah, Dad. I'm okay. You, uh, you know Adrik?"

"Yes. Hello. Um, you got some paint on your, uh, suit there, buddy," her father pointed out, his eyebrows raised all the way to his hairline.

I looked down and shook my head.

"Yes, well, I will fix that once I get Sofia back home," I said.

"What? I am home," she whispered, her velvet eyes tearing up as she tried unsuccessfully to retreat.

"No, no Zaika moya. This is not home. This is your family's home, yes. But not your home."

"You said one month. It's over, you were gone—"

"Technically, I have four days left."

Her tears spilled down her face, and they were killing me. God, she was killing me. So beautiful. So perfect. How did she not know? She struggled against my hold, but I pressed her harder into the wall, getting paint all over her back.

"Is that what you want, then? Four days? Then I leave and have to feel all this again? No. You can't ask me to do that," she said, hiccupping on a sob as she tried to turn away from me.

"No, I don't want you for four days. I said this is not your home, and you know damn well it isn't."

"What are you talking about? Can't you see how much this is hurting me?"

"I see it, Zaika, and I don't understand why you don't know what I am saying."

"Because, you fuck, you haven't said anything yet!" Sofia yelled and kicked at me with her sneaker clad feet, her velvet eyes flashing molten fire at me.

"What do you want to know?" I asked.

"Where were you? What happened? What the hell is going on?" she asked.

I couldn't help myself, I kissed her again, loving the feel of her ready submission as she melted in my arms and tangled her tongue with mine. Of course, a second later I was cursing roundly when she bit me. I grinned, licking my lip, and tasting the blood she drew. My cock throbbed with the need to have her.

There she was. My spitfire. My moonlight goddess covered in paint. My fierce little bunny. Zaika moya.

"I had to go fix things with the company. When I was gone, I discovered the truth about everything. You see, Castle was technically the owner of Core-Tech, but really, it was Missy's project. She promised the company to many people, many companies with foreign interests," he explained,

"So, she is the real power and Matthew was just the figurehead," Sofia said.

"Was the real power. Volkov Industries initiated a hostile takeover after your attempted kidnapping. Word of that had already spread, and I could allow no one to think that was acceptable. Still, it didn't sit well with some friends across the sea, my takeover of Castle Corp, and they attempted to steal several of my mines from me. I had to get them back to assure my place as head of this company and to let my enemies know that anyone coming after what is mine will not have a happy ending."

"I see. So, do they know that now? Your enemies?" she asked.

I nodded my head. They knew. The men I had killed myself were still being delivered around the world. In pieces. A message to my enemies not to fuck with the Dark Wolf or anything he claimed as his, and that included Zaika moya.

"So, you're safe now? Your company, and everything," she asked, and I was touched by her concern for me. Not many people asked if I was okay. In fact, no one did. It was new and different, and part of the reason this woman had bewitched me so.

"Come home with me," I whispered, brushing my nose against hers. "Not for four days," I added, when I felt her reticence. "I don't want four days, Zaika, I want forever. This is not your home. I am."

"What?" she asked, eyes filled with tears and her voice laced with wonder.

Fuck, she smelled so good. Beneath the paint, her jasmine scented skin tempted me, called to me like a siren song.

"You belong with me. My Zaika. My Sofia. Come home. Come back. Stay with me. I want you with me, to be mine always."

"What are you saying?"

"I. Am. Your. Home. Zaika moya, I am your home, and you are mine. Don't tell me no. Tell me yes. Say yes," I begged.

No, I didn't care that we were covered in paint inside a cold building in North Bergen while I confessed just how obsessed I was with this woman. And I didn't give a fuck that my brother and Josef, Andres, and her father had front row seats to all my pleading.

"Yes," she said, and I blinked, thinking I hallucinated. "Yes, Adrik. I'll stay with you. I love you."

I crushed her to me then, kissing her long and deep. I picked her up, put her over my shoulder and shouted in Russian, a victory cry. I put her in the car, buckled her up and jumped behind the wheel.

"Where are we going?" she asked, eyes wide as she held onto the dashboard.

Silly Zaika, I would never hurt a hair on her head, especially not while I was driving. She was so fucking adorable. I couldn't wait to get her home, and naked, very naked—*which was where I planned to keep her for a very long time.*

"Home," I said.

EPILOGUE ONE
SOFIA

One month. It all started with a deal for one month of my time, but there I was, six months later, lying half across my sexy husband's—yes, we tied the knot—body.

I traced the lines of the tattoo he'd gotten above his heart, a gothic rose with our names entwined in an infinity symbol in the same style as his other tattoos. It was so fucking sexy, I practically drooled when he'd come home with it.

Stroking my hand across his massive chest, I grinned at the enormous sapphire ring that glittered under the moonlight filtering in from the windows. It was perfect and stunning, but I would have loved anything he placed on my finger to claim me as his.

We lived in the mansion on the Long Island

Sound, which was an absolutely wonderful place to write. I'd decided against traditional publishing and had now released my second novel in a romance series set amongst New York City's fictional elite. It was going well, and I loved what I was doing.

As for Adrik, he'd been working hard as usual. But he left Volkov Towers to his brother and the team of well-trained staff they had working for them. Being a billionaire came with perks, and being able to work from home was one of them.

"Your thoughts are loud, Zaika moya. Want to share?"

I smiled against his chest and kissed his flat nipple, sliding over him until both my legs opened, pressing my core against his stomach. He groaned and reached down with his large hands to cup my ass.

"I was just thinking how this all started with a one month agreement," I said, lowering my face so I could nuzzle his lips.

"Mmm, that first night at the party when I saw you bathed in silver moonlight like a goddess come to life, I knew you were meant for me," he growled against my mouth.

"Then why did you ask me for just a month?"

"Because in all my wildest dreams, Zaika, I could

not imagine ever deserving a woman like you in my life permanently."

"Adrik," I moaned, my sex dripping now with want as he massaged my back, my hips, and my ass.

"But now that I have you," he growled, licking a trail from my neck to my breasts as he switched our positions, putting me on the bottom. "I will never let you go. You are mine. Say it," he commanded.

My entire body heated with desire for him, and I tugged on his hair, pushing him down where I wanted him the most. Adrik chuckled, his chest reverberating with the sound as he kissed and licked my belly, my thighs, and my mons.

"Please," I begged, needing him to just lick me already.

"Say it, Zaika, or this is all you get," he grunted, spreading my folds, and placing a chaste kiss on my lips.

"I'm yours," I moaned, arching my back.

"Again."

"Yours! I'm yours," I said louder.

"Whose?"

"Oh, God, I belong to you, my Dark Wolf. I am yours," I said, leaning up on my elbows.

His eyes glittered like obsidian, and I knew how much he liked it when I claimed to belong to him, my Dark Wolf, out loud and with all the pride I felt. Adrik made that deep, growling noise I loved, the one that said he was pleased and so fucking hungry for me. Then he opened his mouth and closed it over my clit, and I couldn't think anymore. I could only feel.

"You are so perfect, Zaika moya. So fucking sweet. So hot and wet for me."

"Always you. Only you," I said and dug my fingers into his hair as he pushed his tongue inside my clenching sex. "I love you, Adrik! I love you so much," I yelled as lights started dancing behind my eyes, my orgasm so close I could taste it.

"I love you, Zaika," he growled, crawling up my body and slamming his cock all the way inside me with one hard thrust. "I. Love. You. Love you so much. Only you. Always you. My Zaika. My moonlight goddess. My wild obsession."

It was the first time he said those exact words to me. Yes, we'd made our vows to one another, got married with both our families surrounding us, but that was the first time he had ever strung those three words together. Once he started, it was like a dam had broken, and he couldn't stop.

"Love you. Love you. Love, love, love!" Adrik

roared as he pushed us both over the edge, coming so hard, I thought we broke the bed.

He kissed me again, demanding more, and I gave it to him. Willingly. Willfully. For as long as he wanted me.

He asked me to stay, and the truth was, I never left. Not all of me, anyway. Adrik Volkov was in my soul. He owned my heart, and I never wanted to be without him.

I never thought I could ever be so happy, so content. But when I had my Zaika by my side, wearing my ring, I knew I had found the one thing a man like me never expected to find.

Peace.

Sofia was my obsession, but she was also the only one who could quiet the beast, tame the wolf that lived inside me. During my lifetime, I had made enemies. I had burned bridges. Destroyed dynasties. And forged my empire in blood, guts, and sweat. I had earned my nickname. And I was grateful now that it struck fear in so many.

Because also, for the first time in my life, I had something worth dying for. Zaika moya was everything to me and I pitied the man or woman who tried to take her from my side.

"Adrik? Are you ready?" she asked, and I looked up to see her smiling, her hands resting on her swollen abdomen.

One year into our new life together and my moonlight goddess gifted me with another present. She smiled at me, growing my child under her heart, and my entire body trembled with the force of my love for this one woman. She'd given me everything, and in return I would do anything for her to make her happy, keep her safe. Anything.

"Always, Zaika. I am always ready for you."

Her velvet eyes heated with passion as she reached up on tiptoe to kiss my lips. It was Christmas time, and we were on our way to Nonna's house. Life was a little complicated, melding my world and hers, but together, we did it. Our love was just that badass.

"Do you want your gift early?" she asked, biting her lip.

I held her hand and led the way to the car that was parked outside, waiting for us. Josef opened the door, and I helped Sofia get inside, making sure I buckled her belt before I moved in beside her.

"What gift?" I asked when I finally sat down,

and her smile widened as she handed me a slip of paper with a large dark circle on it and a tiny glowing shape I could almost make out as a tiny human.

"What is this?"

"That's your daughter," she said, tears in her eyes as she gave me the greatest gift of all.

A sound escaped my lips, part groan, part sob, part cheer. Then I turned to her, wrapping my arms around her and I vowed to her again to always be there, to protect, to love, to worship.

"I love you, Zaika moya."

"I love you too, Adrik. Only you."

And I knew then there was no getting rid of this obsession. It was only getting bigger from here on out.

T*he end.*

Did you enjoy this contemporary romance book?
Please consider dropping a line or two in a review so other
readers can enjoy it, too.

Look for the next book in the series, His Wild Temptation, featuring Adrik's brother, Marat Volkov.

Want more Wild Billionaire Books? Visit my website for more: https://www.cdgorri.com/series/wild-billionaire-romance
Thank you and happy reading!

del mare alla stella,
C.D. Gorri

P.S. Indie authors like me count on word of mouth to get my books seen, so if you have a blog or a social media account and you want to post about my books, be sure to include #cdgorribooks so I can see it and I will share to too. THANK YOU.

His Wild
TEMPTATION
A WILD BILLIONAIRE ROMANCE 2
USA TODAY BESTSELLING AUTHOR
C.D. GORRI

READING ON A BUDGET?

Hello Readers!

I am so excited to be able to offer you exclusive bundles available only on CDGORRI.COM for readers using my BUY DIRECT option.

Right now, I have several bundles available at a whopping 30% off the listed prices and there are several series bundles to choose from.

Orders will be delivered via BookFunnel email. Just download to your favorite app and READ!

Thank you for buying direct. Have an awesome day!

xoxo,

C.D. Gorri

Merciful Lies by C.D. Gorri

Lies can be merciful. It just depends on the why.

Meredith

I knew the second I saw him, my life would change forever. When my brother offers me as payment to Nico Fury, the king of the Vipers, how can I refuse? Tattooed, built, and tall, he was the only man I saw when I walked into the room. It was like he occupied all the available space, sitting on his throne of blood, sweat, and lies.

Nerves assailed me, but I owed my brother too much to let anything happen to him. One night. That was all. But it would leave me wrecked. Actions always had consequences. Six months later, my brother was killed by a rival organization, and now they were after me.

There was only one place I could go to keep my unborn baby safe. I just hoped the king would be merciful.

***

Nico

Perfect things didn't exist, at least not in my experience. But she was pretty close. I had her in my bed for one night, and I couldn't shake the memory. No, I wasn't meant to keep soft things like Meredith Keller. My life belonged to my crew, and we were a vicious group. Hell, we weren't called Vipers for nothing.

But she was different. She made me want, and I loved and hated her for it. Meredith was light in a world of constant darkness. She was all warmth and beauty like no other. And I craved her like a drug. Six months had passed since I took her in return for clearing her brother's debt to me, but that man attracted trouble like honey did flies. It wasn't long before I learned Sam Keller had gotten himself killed. Less than an hour later, Meredith came back to me, on her knees, asking for sanctuary.

I knew the moment I saw the swell of her stomach she was carrying my baby. Meredith thought coming here would protect her, but she was walking right into the Viper's nest. Before I was finished, my little runaway would be begging me for mercy.

Merciful Lies is the first in the contemporary

romance series of connected standalones, Jersey Bad Boys. This series features familiar tropes such as enemies to lovers, forced proximity, arranged marriages, secret babies, and contains some violence and explicit scenes.

EXCERPT FROM HIS CARROT HER MUFFIN

I had one stop to make before driving all the way back to Kent Township in Sussex County, New Jersey. We were supposed to get another freaking snowstorm right on Christmas Eve, too. Luckily, that wasn't for another couple of days. The roads were clear, for now.

I walked into the apartment I shared with my best friend, Kelsey. She was working out in the middle of the living room, Pilates, yoga, some combo of the two, I did not know. I shook my head as she bent her long, thin frame with the expertise of a professional contortionist.

"You're back," she said, popping upright like she was on a sugar high, and I had to bite my tongue to stop myself from screaming in surprise.

"Just for a second, Kels. I'm just grabbing my suitcase."

"Okay, well, drive safely, and remember, it's okay to feel when you are back there," she said, big blue eyes keen.

"Geez, Kelsey, I have feelings," I grumbled.

"Yeah, sweetie, but you've been walking around like a robot ever since Dale," she paused, wincing when I turned to face her.

"We said we would not mention his name. We made a vow!" I growled.

Dale was my latest failed relationship. He worked in the same office we did for an advertising firm in Manhattan. I hated my job. I felt slimy when I worked on campaigns that were clearly misleading the populace.

Maybe I needed a whole life makeover…

Read more www.cdgorri.com/books/his-carrot-her-muffin

The Maverick Pride Tales:

Dire Wolf Mates:

Wyvern Protection Unit:

Jersey Sure Shifters/EveL Worlds:

The Guardians of Chaos:

Twice Mated Tales

Hearts of Stone Series

Moongate Island Tales

Mated in Hope Falls

Speed Dating with the Denizens of the Underworld

Hungry Fur Love

Island Stripe Pride

NYC Shifter Tales

A Howlin' Good Fairytale Retelling

Standalones:

Witch Shifter Clan

Young Adult/Urban Fantasy Books

The Grazi Kelly Novel Series

The Angela Tanner Files

G'Witches Magical Mysteries Series

Co-written with P. Mattern

Witches of Westwood Academy

with Gina Kincade

<u>Be sure to check out my BUY DIRECT BUNDLES</u> and get 30% off when you buy available only my website.

USA Today Bestselling author C.D. Gorri writes paranormal and contemporary romance and urban fantasy books with plenty of steam and humor.

Join her mailing list here: https://www.cdgorri.com/newsletter

An avid reader with a profound love for books and literature, she is usually found with a book in hand. C.D. lives in her home state, New Jersey, where many of her characters and stories are based. Her tales are fast-paced yet detailed with satisfying conclusions. If you enjoy powerful heroines and loyal heroes who face relatable problems in supernatural settings, journey into the Grazi Kelly Universe today.

You will find sassy, curvy heroines and sexy, love-driven heroes who find their HEAs between the pages.

Wolves, Bears, Dragons, Tigers, Witches, Vampires, and tons more Shifters and supernatural creatures dwell within her paranormal works. The most important thing is every mate in this universe is fated, loyal, and true lovers always get their happily-ever-afters.

In her contemporary works, you will find fiercely possessive men and the smart, confident, curvy women they are crazy about. As always, the HEA is between the pages.

Thank you and happy reading!
del mare alla stella,
C.D. Gorri

http://www.cdgorri.com
https://www.facebook.com/Cdgorribooks
https://www.bookbub.com/authors/c-d-gorri
https://twitter.com/cgor22
https://instagram.com/cdgorri/

https://www.goodreads.com/cdgorri
https://www.tiktok.com/@cdgorriauthor